PENGUIN BOOKS

ELEVEN

Patricia Highsmith was born in Fort Worth, Texas, in 1921. Her parents moved to New York when she was six, and she attended the Julia Richmond High School and Barnard College. In her senior years she edited the school magazine, having decided at the age of sixteen to become a writer. Her first novel, *Strangers on a Train*, was filmed by Alfred Hitchcock, and her third, *The Talented Mr Ripley*, was awarded the Edgar Allan Poe Scroll by the Mystery Writers of America. She has commented that she is 'interested in the effect of guilt on my heroes'. Miss Highsmith enjoys gardening and carpentering, painting and sculpture; some of her works have been exhibited. She now lives in Switzerland.

Patricia Highsmith's books include *Deep Water, A Dog's Ransom, The Cry of the Owl, The Glass Cell, Ripley Underground, A Suspension of Mercy, This Sweet Sickness, Ripley's Game, Edith's Diary, The Boy Who Followed Ripley* and several collections of short stories, *The Animal-Lover's Book of Beastly Murder, Little Tales of Misogyny, The Black House, Slowly, Slowly in the Wind* and *People Who Knock on the Door*.

With a Foreword by Graham Greene

Eleven

Patricia Highsmith

Penguin Books

Penguin Books Ltd, Harmondsworth, Middlesex, England
Viking Penguin Inc., 40 West 23rd Street, New York, New York 10010, U.S.A.
Penguin Books Australia Ltd, Ringwood, Victoria, Australia
Penguin Books Canada Ltd, 2801 John Street, Markham, Ontario, Canada L3R 1B4
Penguin Books (N.Z.) Ltd, 182–190 Wairau Road, Auckland 10, New Zealand

First published by William Heinemann Ltd 1970
Published in Penguin Books 1972
Reprinted 1980 (twice), 1984, 1985

'The Birds Poised to Fly', 'The Terrapin', 'Mrs Afton, among Thy Green Braes'
(as 'The Gracious, Pleasant Life of Mrs Afton'), Another Bridge to Cross' and
'The Empty Birdhouse' all originally appeared in *Ellery Queen's Mystery
Magazine*; 'The Snail-Watcher' originally appeared in *Gamma*; 'When the Fleet
Was In at Mobile' originally appeared in *London Life*; 'The Quest for *Blank
Claveringi*' originally appeared in slightly altered form in the *Saturday Evening
Post* as 'The Snails'; 'The Cries of Love' originally appeared in *Women's
Journal*; 'The Heroine' originally appeared in *Harper's Bazaar*; and 'The
Barbarians', Copyright © P. Highsmith and Agence Bradley, 1968, was
originally published in French in No. 17 of *La Revue de Poche*, published by
Robert Laffont, and in English in *Best Mystery Stories* edited by Maurice
Richardson, copyright Introduction and Selection by Faber & Faber, 1968.

Printed and bound in Great Britain by
Cox & Wyman Ltd, Reading
Typeset in Linotype Granjon

For ALEX SZOGYI

CONTENTS

Foreword
by Graham Greene

Miss Highsmith is a crime novelist whose books one can reread many times. There are very few of whom one can say that. She is a writer who has created a world of her own – a world claustrophobic and irrational which we enter each time with a sense of personal danger, with the head half turned over the shoulder, even with a certain reluctance, for these are cruel pleasures we are going to experience, until somewhere about the third chapter the frontier is closed behind us, we cannot retreat, we are doomed to live till the story's end with another of her long series of wanted men.

It makes the tension worse that we are never sure whether even the worst of them, like the talented Mr Ripley, won't get away with it or that the relatively innocent won't suffer like the blunderer Walter on the relatively guilty escape altogether like Sydney Bartleby in *A Suspension of Mercy*. This is a world without moral endings. It has nothing in common with the heroic world of her peers, Hammett and Chandler, and her detectives (sometimes monsters of cruelty like the American Lieutenant Corby of *The Blunderer* or dull sympathetic rational characters like the British Inspector Brockway) have nothing in common with the romantic and disillusioned private eyes who will always, we know, triumph finally over evil and see that justice is done, even though they may have to send a mistress to the chair.

Nothing is certain when we have crossed *this* frontier. It is not the world as we once believed we knew it, but it is frighteningly more real to us than the house next door. Actions are sudden and impromptu and the motives sometimes so inexplicable that we simply have to accept them on trust. I believe because it is impossible. Her characters are irrational, and they leap to life in their very lack of reason; suddenly we realize how unbelievably rational most fictional characters are as they lead their lives from A to Z, like commuters always taking the same train. The motives of these characters are never inexplicable because they are so drearily obvious. The characters are as flat as a mathematical symbol. We accepted them as real once, but when we look back at them from Miss Highsmith's side of the frontier, we realize that our world was not really as rational as all that. Suddenly with a sense of fear we think, 'Perhaps I really belong *here*,' and going out into the familiar street we pass with a shiver of apprehension the offices of the American Express, the centre, for so many of Miss Highsmith's dubious men, of their rootless European experience, where letters are to be picked up (though the name on the envelope is probably false) and travellers' cheques are to be cashed (with a forged signature).

Miss Highsmith's short stories do not let us down, though we may be able sometimes to brush them off more easily because of their brevity. We haven't lived with them long enough to be totally absorbed. Miss Highsmith is the poet of apprehension rather than fear. Fear after a time, as we all learned in the blitz, is narcotic, it can lull one by fatigue into sleep, but apprehension nags at the nerves gently and inescapably. We have to learn to live with it. Miss Highsmith's finest novel to my mind is *The Tremor of Forgery*, and if I were to be asked what it is about I would reply, 'Apprehension'.

In her short stories Miss Highsmith has naturally to adopt a different method. She is after the quick kill rather than the slow encirclement of the reader, and how admirably and with what field-craft she hunts us down. Some of these stories were written twenty years ago, before her first novel, *Strangers on a Train*, but we have no sense that she is learning her craft by false starts, by trial and error. 'The Heroine', published nearly a quarter of a century ago, is as much a study of apprehension as her last novel. We can feel how dangerous (and irrational) the young nurse is from her first interview. We want to cry to the parents, 'Get rid of her before it's too late'.

My own favourite in this collection is the story 'When the Fleet Was In at Mobile' with the moving horror of its close here is Miss Highsmith at her claustrophobic best. 'The Terrapin', a late Highsmith, is a cruel story of childhood which can bear comparison with Saki's masterpiece, 'Sredni Vashtar', and for pure physical horror, which is an emotion rarely evoked by Miss Highsmith, 'The Snail-Watcher' would be hard to beat. Mr Knoppert has the same attitude to his snails as Miss Highsmith to human beings. He watches them with the same emotionless curiosity as Miss Highsmith watches the talented Mr Ripley:

Mr Knoppert had wandered into the kitchen one evening for a bite of something before dinner, and had happened to notice that a couple of snails in the china bowl on the draining board were behaving very oddly. Standing more or less on their tails, they were weaving before each other for all the world like a pair of snakes hypnotized by a flute player. A moment later, their faces came together in a kiss of voluptuous intensity. Mr Knoppert bent closer and studied them from all angles. Something else was happening: a protuberance like an ear was appearing on the right side of the head of both snails. His instinct told him that he was watching a sexual activity of some sort.

G. G.

The Snail-Watcher

When Mr Peter Knoppert began to make a hobby of snail-watching, he had no idea that his handful of specimens would become hundreds in no time. Only two months after the original snails were carried up to the Knoppert study, some thirty glass tanks and bowls, all teeming with snails, lined the walls, rested on the desk and windowsills, and were beginning even to cover the floor. Mrs Knoppert disapproved strongly, and would no longer enter the room. It smelled, she said, and besides she had once stepped on a snail by accident, a horrible sensation she would never forget. But the more his wife and friends deplored his unusual and vaguely repellent pastime, the more pleasure Mr Knoppert seemed to find in it.

'I never cared for nature before in my life,' Mr Knoppert often remarked – he was a partner in a brokerage firm, a man who had devoted all his life to the science of finance – 'but snails have opened my eyes to the beauty of the animal world.'

If his friends commented that snails were not really animals, and their slimy habitats hardly the best example of the beauty of nature, Mr Knoppert would tell them with a superior smile that they simply didn't know all that he knew about snails.

And it was true. Mr Knoppert had witnessed an exhibition that was not described, certainly not adequately described, in any encyclopaedia or zoology book that he had been able to find. Mr Knoppert had wandered into the kitchen one evening for a bite of something before dinner, and had happened to notice that a couple of snails in the china bowl on the draining board were behaving very oddly. Standing more or less on their tails, they were weaving before each other for all the world like a pair of snakes hypnotized by a flute player. A moment later, their faces came together in a kiss of voluptuous intensity. Mr Knoppert bent closer and studied them from all angles. Something else was happening: a protuberance like an ear was appearing on the right side of the head of both snails. His instinct told him that he was watching a sexual activity of some sort.

The cook came in and said something to him, but Mr Knoppert silenced her with an impatient wave of his hand. He couldn't take his eyes from the enchanted little creatures in the bowl.

When the ear-like excrescences were precisely together rim to rim, a whitish rod like another small tentacle shot out from one ear and arched over toward the ear of the other snail. Mr Knoppert's first surmise was dashed when a tentacle sallied from the other snail, too. Most peculiar, he thought. The two tentacles withdrew, then came forth again, and as if they had found some invisible mark, remained fixed in either snail. Mr Knoppert peered intently closer. So did the cook.

'Did you ever see anything like this?' Mr Knoppert asked.

'No. They must be fighting,' the cook said indifferently and went away. That was a sample of the ignorance on the subject of snails that he was later to discover everywhere.

Mr Knoppert continued to observe the pair of snails off and on for more than an hour, until first the ears, then the rods, withdrew, and the snails themselves relaxed their attitudes and paid no further attention to each other. But by that time, a different pair of snails had begun a flirtation, and were slowly rearing themselves to get into a position for kissing. Mr Knoppert told the cook that the snails were not to be served that evening. He took the bowl of them up to his study. And snails were never again served in the Knoppert household.

That night, he searched his encyclopaedias and a few general science books he happened to possess, but there was absolutely nothing on snails' breeding habits, though the oyster's dull reproductive cycle was described in detail. Perhaps it hadn't been a mating he had seen after all, Mr Knoppert decided after a day or two. His wife Edna told him either to eat the snails or get rid of them – it was at this time that she stepped upon a snail that had crawled out on to the floor – and Mr Knoppert might have, if he hadn't come across a sentence in Darwin's *Origin of Species* on a page given to gastropoda. The sentence was in French, a language Mr Knoppert did not know, but the word *sensualité* made him tense like a bloodhound that has suddenly found the scent. He was in the public library at that time, and laboriously he translated the sentence with the aid of a French-English dictionary. It was a statement of less than a hundred words, saying that snails manifested a sensuality in their mating that was not to be found elsewhere in the animal kingdom. That was all. It was from the notebooks of Henri Fabre. Obviously Darwin had decided not to translate it for the average reader, but to leave it in its original language for the scholarly few who really cared. Mr Knoppert considered himself one of the scholarly few now, and his round, pink face beamed with self-esteem.

He had learned that his snails were the freshwater type that laid their eggs in sand or earth, so he put moist earth and a little saucer of water into a big wash-bowl and transferred his snails into it. Then he waited for something to happen. Not even another mating happened. He picked up the snails one by one and looked at them, without seeing anything suggestive of pregnancy. But one snail he couldn't pick up. The shell might have been glued to the earth. Mr Knoppert suspected the snail had buried its head in the ground to die. Two more days went by, and on the morning of the third, Mr Knoppert found a spot of crumbly earth where the snail had been. Curious, he investigated the crumbles with a match stem, and to his delight discovered a pit full of shiny new eggs. Snail eggs! He hadn't been wrong. Mr Knoppert called his wife and the cook to look at them. The eggs looked very much like big caviar, only they were white instead of black or red.

'Well, naturally they have to breed some way,' was his

wife's comment. Mr Knoppert couldn't understand her lack of interest. He had to go and look at the eggs every hour that he was at home. He looked at them every morning to see if any change had taken place, and the eggs were his last thought every night before he went to bed. Moreoever, another snail was now digging a pit. And another pair of snails was mating! The first batch of eggs turned a greyish colour, and miniscule spirals of shells became discernible on one side of each egg. Mr Knoppert's anticipation rose to a higher pitch. At last a morning arrived – the eighteenth after laying, according to Mr Knoppert's careful count – when he looked down into the egg pit and saw the first tiny moving head, the first stubby little antennae uncertainly exploring the nest. Mr Knoppert was as happy as the father of a new child. Every one of the seventy or more eggs in the pit came miraculously to life. He had seen the entire reproductive cycle evolve to a successful conclusion. And the fact that no one, at least no one that he knew of, was acquainted with a fraction of what he knew, lent his knowledge a thrill of discovery, the piquancy of the esoteric. Mr Knoppert made notes on successive matings and egg hatchings. He narrated snail biology to fascinated, more often shocked, friends and guests, until his wife squirmed with embarrassment.

'But where is it going to stop, Peter? If they keep on reproducing at this rate, they'll take over the house!' his wife told him after fifteen or twenty pits had hatched.

'There's no stopping nature,' he replied good-humouredly. 'They've only taken over the study. There's plenty of room there.'

So more and more glass tanks and bowls were moved in. Mr Knoppert went to the market and chose several of the more lively-looking snails, and also a pair he found mating, unobserved by the rest of the world. More and more egg pits appeared in the dirt floors of the tanks, and out of each pit crept finally from seventy to ninety baby snails, transparent as dewdrops, gliding up rather than down the strips of fresh lettuce that Mr Knoppert was quick to give all the pits as edible ladders for the climb. Mating went on so often that he no longer bothered to watch them. A mating could last twenty-four hours. But the thrill of seeing the white caviar become shells and start to move – that never diminished however often he witnessed it.

His colleagues in the brokerage office noticed a new zest for life in Peter Knoppert. He became more daring in his moves, more brilliant in his calculations, became in fact a little vicious in his schemes, but he brought money in for his company. By unanimous vote, his basic salary was raised from forty to sixty thousand dollars per year. When anyone congratulated him on his achievements, Mr Knoppert gave all the credit to his snails and the beneficial relaxation he derived from watching them.

He spent all his evenings with his snails in the room that was no longer a study but a kind of aquarium. He loved to strew the tanks with fresh lettuce and pieces of boiled potato and beet, then turn on the sprinkler system that he had installed in the tanks to simulate natural rainfall. Then all the snails would liven up and begin eating, mating, or merely gliding through the shallow water with obvious pleasure. Mr Knoppert often let a snail crawl on to his forefinger – he fancied his snails enjoyed this human contact – and he would feed it a piece of lettuce by hand, would observe the snail from all sides, finding as much aesthetic satisfaction as another man might from contemplating a Japanese print.

By now, Mr Knoppert did not allow anyone to set foot in his study. Too many snails had the habit of crawling around on the floor, of going to sleep glued to chair bottoms, and to the backs of books on the shelves. Snails spent much of their time sleeping, especially the older snails. But there were enough less indolent snails who preferred love-making. Mr Knoppert estimated that about a dozen pairs of snails must be kissing all the time. And certainly there was a multitude of baby and adolescent snails. They were impossible to count. But Mr Knoppert did count the snails sleeping and creeping on the ceiling alone, and arrived at something between eleven and twelve hundred.

The tanks, the bowls, the underside of his desk and the book-shelves must surely have held fifty times that number. Mr Knoppert meant to scrape the snails off the ceiling one day soon. Some of them had been up there for weeks, and he was afraid they were not taking in enough nourishment. But of late he had been a little too busy, and too much in need of the tranquillity that he got simply from sitting in the study in his favourite chair.

During the month of June he was so busy he often worked late into the evening at his office. Reports were piling in at the end of the fiscal year. He made calculations, spotted a half-dozen possibilities of gain, and reserved the most daring, the least obvious moves for his private operations. By this time next year, he thought, he should be three or four times as well off as now. He saw his bank account multiplying as easily and rapidly as his snails. He told his wife this, and she was over-joyed. She even forgave him the ruination of the study, and the stale, fishy smell that was spreading throughout the whole upstairs.

'Still, I do wish you'd take a look just to see if anything's happening, Peter,' she said to him rather anxiously one morning. 'A tank might have overturned or something, and I wouldn't want the rug to be spoilt. You haven't been in the study for nearly a week, have you?'

Mr Knoppert hadn't been in for nearly two weeks. He didn't tell his wife that the rug was pretty much gone already. I'll go up tonight,' he said.

But it was three more days before he found time. He went in one evening just before bedtime and was surprised to find the floor quite covered with snails, with three or four layers of snails. He had difficulty closing the door without mashing any. The dense clusters of snails in the corners made the room look positively round, as if he stood inside some huge, conglomerate stone. Mr Knoppert cracked his knuckles and gazed around him in astonishment. They had not only covered every surface, but thousands of snails hung down into the room from the chandelier in a grotesque clump.

Mr Knoppert felt for the back of a chair to steady himself. He felt only a lot of shells under his hand. He had to smile a little: there were snails in the chair seat, piled up on one another, like a lumpy cushion. He really must do something about the ceiling, and immediately. He took an umbrella from the corner, brushed some of the snails off it, and cleared a place on his desk to stand. The umbrella point tore the wallpaper, and then the weight of the snails pulled down a long strip that hung almost to the floor. Mr Knoppert felt suddenly frustrated and angry. The sprinklers would make them move. He pulled the lever.

The sprinklers came on in all the tanks, and the seething activity of the entire room increased at once. Mr Knoppert slid his feet along the floor, through tumbling snails' shells that made a sound like pebbles on a beach, and directed a couple of the sprinklers at the ceiling. This was a mistake, he saw at once. The softened paper began to tear, and he dodged one slowly falling mass only to be hit by a swinging festoon of snails, really hit quite a stunning blow on the side of the head. He went down on one knee, dazed. He should open a window, he thought, the air was stifling. And there were snails crawling over his shoes and up his trouser legs. He shook his feet irritably. He was just going to the door, intending to call for one of the servants to help him, when the chandelier fell on him. Mr Knoppert sat down heavily on the floor. He saw now that he couldn't possibly get a window open, because the snails were fastened thick and deep over the windowsills. For a moment, he felt he couldn't get up, felt as if he were suffocating. It was not only the musty smell of the room, but everywhere he looked long wallpaper strips covered with snails blocked his vision as if he were in a prison.

'Edna!' he called, and was amazed at the muffled, ineffectual sound of his voice. The room might have been soundproof.

He crawled to the door, heedless of the sea of snails he crushed under hands and knees. He could not get the door open. There were so many snails on it, crossing and recrossing the crack of the door on all sides, they actually resisted his strength.

'Edna!' A snail crawled into his mouth. He spat it out in disgust. Mr Knoppert tried to brush the snails off his arms. But for every hundred he dislodged, four hundred seemed to slide upon him and fasten to him again, as if they deliberately sought him out as the only comparatively snail-free surface in the room. There were snails crawling over his eyes. Then just as he staggered to his feet, something else hit him – Mr Knoppert couldn't even see what. He was fainting! At any rate, he was on the floor. His arms felt like leaden weights as he tried to reach his nostrils, his eyes, to free them from the sealing, murderous snail bodies.

'Help!' He swallowed a snail. Choking, he widened his mouth for air and felt a snail crawl over his lips on to his tongue. He was in hell! He could feel them gliding over his legs like a glutinous river, pinning his legs to the floor. 'Ugh!' Mr Knoppert's breath came in feeble gasps. His vision grew black, a horrible, undulating black. He could not breathe at all, because he could not reach his nostrils, could not move his hands. Then through the slit of one eye, he saw directly in front of him, only inches away, what had been, he knew, the rubber plant that stood in its pot near the door. A pair of snails were quietly making love in it. And right beside them, tiny snails as pure as dewdrops were emerging from a pit like an infinite army into their widening world.

The Birds Poised to Fly

Every morning, Don looked into his mailbox, but there was never a letter from her.

She hadn't had time, he would say to himself. He went over all the things she had to do – transport her belongings from Rome to Paris, settle into an apartment which she had presumably found in Paris before she made the move, probably work a few days at her new job before she found time and inspiration to answer his letter. But finally the greatest number of days to which he could stretch all this had come and gone. And three more days had passed, and still there was no letter from her.

She's waiting to make up her mind,' he told himself. 'Naturally, she wants to be sure about how she feels before she puts a word down on paper.'

He had written to Rosalind thirteen days ago that he loved her and wanted to marry her. That was perhaps a bit hasty in view of a short courtship, but Don thought he had written a good letter, not putting pressure, simply stating what he felt. After all, he had known Rosalind two years, or rather met her in New York two years ago. He had seen her again in Europe last month, and he was in love with her and wanted to marry her.

Since his return from Europe three weeks ago, he had seen only one or two of his friends. He had quite enough to occupy himself in making plans about himself and Rosalind. Rosalind was an industrial designer, and she liked Europe. If she preferred to stay in Europe, Don could arrange to live there, too. His French was fairly good now. His company, Dirksen and Hall, consulting engineers, even had a branch in Paris. It could all be quite simple. Just a visa for him to take some things over, like books and carpets and his record player, some tools and drawing instruments, and he could make the move. Don felt that he hadn't yet taken full stock of his happiness. Each day was like the lifting a little higher of a curtain that revealed a magnificent landscape. He wanted Rosalind to be with him when he could finally see all of it. There was really only one thing that kept him from a happy, positive rush into that landscape now: the fact that he hadn't even a letter from her to take with him. He wrote again to Rome and put a 'Please forward' in Italian on the envelope. She was probably in Paris by now, but she had no doubt left a forwarding address in Rome.

Two more days passed, and still there was no letter. There was only a letter from his mother in California, an advertisement from a local liquor shop, and some kind of bulletin about a primary election. He smiled a little, snapped his mailbox to and locked it, and strode off to work. It never made him feel sad, the instant when he discovered there was no letter. It was rather a funny kind of shock, as if she had played a guileless little trick on him and was withholding her letter one more day. Then the realization of the nine hours before him, until he could come home and see if a special delivery notice had arrived, descended on him like a burden, and quite suddenly he felt tired and spiritless. Rosalind wouldn't write him a special delivery, not after all this time. There was never anything to do but wait until the next morning.

He saw a letter in the box the next morning. But it was an announcement of an art show. He tore it into tiny pieces and crushed them in his fist.

In the box next to his, there were three letters. They had been there since yesterday morning, he remembered. Who was this fellow Dusenberry who didn't bother collecting his mail?

That morning in the office, an idea came to him that raised his spirits: her letter might have been put into the box next to his by mistake. The mailman opened all the boxes at once, in a row, and at least once Don had found a letter for someone else in his own box. He began to feel optimistic: her letter would say that she loved him, too. How could she not say it, when they had been so happy together in Juan-les-Pins? He would cable her, I love you, I love you. No, he would telephone, because her letter would have her Paris address, possibly her office address also, and he would know where to reach her.

When he had met Rosalind two years ago in New York, they had gone out to dinner and to the theatre two or three times. Then she hadn't accepted his next invitations, so Don had supposed there was another man in the picture whom she liked better. It hadn't mattered very much to him at that time. But when he had met her by accident in Juan-les-Pins, things had been quite different. It had been love at second sight. The proof of it was that Rosalind had got free of three people she was with, another girl and two men, had let them go on without her to Cannes, and she had stayed with him at Juan-les-Pins. They had had a perfect five days together, and Don had said, 'I love you,' and Rosalind had said it once, too. But they hadn't made plans about the future, or even talked about when they might see each other again. How could he have been so stupid! He wished he had asked her to go to bed with him, for that matter. But on the other hand, his emotions had been so much more serious. Any two people could have an affair on a holiday. To be in love and want to marry was something else. He had assumed, from her behaviour, that she felt the same way. Rosalind was cool, smiling, brunette, not tall, but she gave the impression of tallness. She was intelligent, would never do anything foolish, Don felt, never anything impulsive. Nor would he ever propose to anyone on impulse. Marriage was something one thought over for some time, weeks, months, maybe a year or so. He felt he had thought over his proposal of marriage for longer than the five days in Juan-les-Pins. He believed that Rosalind Farnes was a girl or a woman (she was twenty-six, and he twenty-nine) of substance, that her work had much in common with his, and that they had every chance of happiness.

That evening, the three letters were still in Dusenberry's box, and Don looked for Dusenberry's bell in the list opposite the mailboxes, and rang it firmly. They might be in, even though they hadn't collected their mail.

No answer.

Dusenberry or the Dusenberrys were away, apparently.

Would the superintendent let him open the box? Certainly not. And the superintendent hadn't the key or keys, anyway.

One of the letters looked like an airmail envelope from Europe. It was maddening. Don put a finger in one of the slits in the polished metal front, and tried to pull the box open. It remained closed. He pushed his own key into the lock and tried to turn it. The lock gave a snap, and the bolt moved, opening the box half an inch. It wouldn't open any farther. Don had his door-keys in his hand, and he stuck one of the doorkeys between the box door and the brass frame and used it as a lever. The brass front bent enough for him to reach the letters. He took the letters and pressed the brass front as straight as he could. None of the letters was for him. He looked at them, trembling like a thief. Then he thrust one into his coat pocket, pushed the others into the bent mailbox, and entered his apartment building. The elevators were around a corner. Don found one empty and ready, and rode up to the third floor alone.

His heart was pounding as he closed his own door. Why had he taken the one letter? He would put it back, of course. It had looked like a personal letter, but it was from America. He looked at its address in fine blue handwriting. R. L. Dusenberry, etc. And at its return address on the back of the envelope: Edith W. Whitcomb, 717 Garfield Drive, Scranton, Pa. Dusenberry's girl friend, he thought at once. It was a fat letter in a square envelope. He ought to put it back now. And the damaged mailbox? Well, there wasn't anything stolen from it, after all. A serious offence, to break a mailbox, but let them hammer it out. As long as nothing was stolen, was it so awful?

Don got a suit from his closet to take to the cleaners, and picked up Dusenberry's letter. But with the letter in his hand, he was suddenly curious to know what was in it. Before he had time to feel shame, he went to the kitchen and put on water to boil. The envelope flap curled back neatly in the steam, and Don was patient. The letter was three pages in longhand, the pages written on both sides.

'Darling,' it began,

I miss you so, I have to write to you. Have you really made up your mind how you feel? You said you thought it would all vanish for both of us. Do you know how I feel? The same way I did the night we stood on the bridge and watched the lights come on in Bennington ...

Don read it through incredulously, and with fascination. The girl was madly in love with Dusenberry. She waited only for him to answer, for merely a sign from him. She spoke of the town in Vermont where they had been, and he wondered if they had met there or gone there together? My God, he thought, if Rosalind would only write him a letter like this! In this case, apparently, Dusenberry wouldn't write to her. From the letter, Dusenberry might not have written once since they had last seen each other. Don sealed the letter with glue, carefully, and put it into his pocket.

The last paragraph repeated itself in his mind:

I didn't think I'd write to you again, but now I've done it. I have to be honest, because that's the way I am.

Don felt that was the way he was, too. The paragraph went on:

Do you remember or have you forgotten, and do you want to see me again or don't you? If I don't hear from you in a few days, I'll know.

My love always,
Edith

He looked at the date on the stamp. The letter had been posted six days ago. He thought of the girl called Edith Whitcomb spinning and stretching out the days, trying to convince herself somehow that the delay was justified. Six days. Yet of course she still hoped. She was hoping this minute down there in Scranton, Pennsylvania. What kind of man was Dusenberry? A Casanova? A married man who wanted to drop a flirtation? Which of the six or eight men he had ever noticed in his building was Dusenberry? A couple of hatless chaps dashing out at 8.30 in the morning? A slower-moving man in a Homburg? Don never paid much attention to his neighbours.

He held his breath, and for an instant he seemed to feel the stab of the girl's own loneliness and imperilled hope, to feel the last desperate flutterings of hope against his own lips. With one word, he could make her so happy. Or rather, Dusenberry could.

'Bastard,' he whispered.

He put the suit down, went to his worktable and wrote on a scrap of paper, 'Edith, I love you.' He liked seeing it written, legible. He felt it settled an important matter that had been precariously balanced before. Don crumpled up the paper and threw it into the waste-basket.

Then he went downstairs and forced the letter back in the box, and dropped his suit at the cleaners. He walked a long way up Second Avenue, grew tired and kept walking until he was at the edge of Harlem, and then he caught a bus downtown. He was hungry, but he couldn't think of anything he wanted to eat. He was thinking, deliberately, of nothing. He was waiting for the night to pass and for morning to bring the next mail delivery. He was thinking, vaguely, of Rosalind. And of the girl in Scranton. A pity people had to suffer so from their emotions. Like himself. For though Rosalind had made him so happy, he couldn't deny that these last three weeks had been a torture. Yes, my God, twenty-two days now! He felt strangely ashamed tonight of admitting it had been twenty-two days. Strangely ashamed? There was nothing strange about it, if he faced it. He felt ashamed of possibly having lost her. He should have told her very definitely in Juan-les-Pins that he not only loved her but wanted to marry her. He might have lost her now because he hadn't.

The thought made him get off the bus. He drove the horrible, deathly possibility out of his mind, kept it out of his mind and out of his flesh by walking.

Suddenly, he had an inspiration. His idea didn't go very far, it hadn't an objective, but it was a kind of project for this evening. He began it on the way home, trying to imagine exactly what Dusenberry would write to Miss Whitcomb if he had read the last letter, and if Dusenberry would write back, not necessarily that he loved her, but that he at least cared enough to want to see her again.

It took him about fifteen minutes to write the leter. He said that he had been silent all this while because he hadn't been sure of his own feelings or of hers. He said he wanted to see her before he told her anything, and asked her when she might be able to see him. He couldn't think of Dusenberry's first name, if the girl had used it at all in her letter, but he remembered the R. L. Dusenberry on the envelope, and signed it simply 'R'.

While he had been writing it, he had not intended actually to send it to her, but as he read the anonymous, typewritten words, he began to consider it. It was so little to give her, and seemed so harmless: when can we see each other? But of course it was futile and false also. Dusenberry obviously didn't care and never would, or he wouldn't have let six days go by. If Dusenberry didn't take up the situation where he left it off, he would be prolonging an unreality. Don stared at the 'R.' and knew that all he wanted was an answer from 'Edith', one single, positive, happy answer. So he wrote below the letter again on the typewriter:

P.S. Could you write to me c/o Dirksen and Hall, Chanin Building, N.Y.C.

He could get the letter somehow, if Edith answered. And if she didn't write in a few days, it would mean that Dusenberry had replied to her. Or if a letter from Edith came, Don could — he would have to — take it on himself to break off the affair as painlessly as possible.

After he posted the letter, he felt completely free of it, and somehow relieved. He slept well, and awakened with a conviction that a letter awaited him in the box downstairs. When he saw that there wasn't one (at least not one from Rosalind, only a telephone bill), he felt a swift and simple disappointment, an exasperation that he had not experienced before. Now there seemed just no reason why he shouldn't have got a letter.

A letter from Scranton was at the office next morning. Don spotted it on the receptionist's desk and took it, and the receptionist was so busy at that moment on the telephone, that there was no question and not even a glance from her.

'My darling,' it began, and he could scarcely bear to read its gush of sentiment, and folded the page up before anyone in the engineering department where he worked could see him reading it. He both liked and disliked having the letter in his pocket. He kept telling himself that he hadn't really expected a letter, but he knew that wasn't true. Why wouldn't she have written? She suggested they go somewhere together next weekend (evidently Dusenberry was as free as the wind), and she asked him to set the time and place.

He thought of her as he worked at his desk, thought of the ardent, palpitating, faceless piece of feminity in Scranton, that he could manipulate with a word. Ironic! And he couldn't even make Rosalind answer him from Paris!

'God!' he whispered, and got up from his desk. He left the office without a word to anyone.

He had just thought of something fatal. It had occured to him that Rosalind might all this time be planning how to break it to him that she didn't love him, that she never could. He could not get the idea out of his mind. Now instead of imagining her happy, puzzled, or secretly pleased face, he saw her frowning over the awkward chore of composing a letter that would break it all off. He felt her pondering the phrases that would do it most gently.

The idea so upset him that he could do nothing that evening. The more he thought about it, the more likely it seemed that she *was* writing to him, or contemplating writing to him, to end it. He could imagine the exact steps by which she might have come to the decision: after the first brief period of missing him, must have come a realization that she could do without him when she was occupied with her job and her friends in Paris, as he knew she must be. Second, the reality of the circumstances that he was in America and she in Europe might have put her off. But above all, perhaps the fact that she had discovered she didn't really love him. This at least must be true, because people simply didn't neglect for so long to write to people they cared about.

Abruptly he stood up, staring at the clock, facing it like a thing he fought. 8.17 p.m., September 15th. He bore its whole weight upon his tense body and his clenched hands. Twenty-five days, so many hours, so many minutes, since his first letter . . . His mind slid from under the weight and fastened on the girl in Scranton. He felt he owed her a reply. He read her letter over again, more carefully, sentimentally lingering over a phrase here and there, as if he cared profoundly about her hopeless and dangling love, almost as if it were his own love. Here was someone who pled with him to tell her a time and a place of meeting. Ardent, eager, a captive of herself only, she was a bird poised to fly. Suddenly, he went to the telephone and dictated a telegram:

Meet me Grand Central Terminal Lexington side Friday 6 p.m. Love, R.

Friday was the day after tomorrow.

Thursday there was still no letter, no letter from Rosalind, and now he had not the courage or perhaps the physical energy to imagine anything about her. There was only his love inside him, undiminished, and heavy as a rock. As soon as he got up Friday morning, he thought of the girl in Scranton. She would be getting up this morning and packing her bag, or if she went to work at all, would move in a dreamworld of Dusenberry all the day.

When he went downstairs, he saw the red and blue border of an airmail envelope in his box, and felt a slow, almost painful shock. He opened the box and dragged the long flimsy envelope out, his hands shaking, dropping his keys at his feet.

The letter was only about fifteen typewritten lines.

Don,

Terribly sorry to have waited so long to answer your letter, but it's been one thing after another here. Only today got settled enough to begin work. Was delayed in Rome first of all, and getting the apartment organized here has been hellish because of strikes of electricians and whatnot.

You are an angel, Don, I know that and I won't forget it. I won't forget our days on the Côte either. But darling, I can't see myself changing my life radically and abruptly either to marry here or anywhere. I can't possibly get to the States Christmas, things are too busy here, and why should you uproot yourself from New York? Maybe by Christmas, maybe by the time you get this, your feelings will have changed a bit.

But will you write me again? And not let this make you unhappy? And can we see each other again some time? Maybe unexpectedly and wonderfully as it was in Juan-les-Pins?

Rosalind

He stuffed the letter into his pocket and plunged out of the door. His thoughts were a chaos, signals of a mortal distress, cries of a silent death, the confused orders of a routed army to rally itself before it was too late, not to give up, not to die.

One thought came through fairly clearly: he had frightened her. His stupid, unrestrained avowal, his torrent of plans had positively turned her against him. If he had said only half as much, she would have known how much he loved her. But he had been specific. He had said, 'Darling, I adore you. Can you come to New York over Christmas? If not, I can fly to Paris. I want to marry you. If you prefer to live in Europe, I'll arrange to live there, too. I can so easily . . . '

What an imbecile he had been!

His mind was already busy at correcting the mistake, already composing the next casual, affectionate letter that would give her some space to breathe in. He would write it this very evening, carefully, and get it exactly right.

Don left the office rather early that afternoon, and was home by a few minutes after 5. The clock reminded him that the girl from Scranton would be at Grand Central at 6 o'clock. He should go and meet her, he thought, though he didn't know why. He certainly wouldn't speak to her. He wouldn't even know her if he saw her, of course. Still, the Grand Central Terminal, rather than the girl, pulled at him like a steady, gentle magnet. He began to change his clothes. He put on his best suit, hesitantly fingered the tie rack, and snatched off a solid blue tie. He felt unsteady and weak, rather as if he were evaporating like the cool sweat that kept forming on his forehead.

He walked downtown toward Forty-second Street.

He saw two or three young women at the Lexington Avenue entrance of the Terminal who might have been Edith W. Whitcomb. He looked for something initialled that they carried, but they had nothing with initials. Then one of the girls met the person she had been waiting for, and suddenly he was sure Edith was the blonde girl in the black cloth coat and the black beret with the military pin. Yes, there was an anxiety in her wide, round eyes that couldn't have come from anything else but the anticipation of someone she loved, and anxiously loved. She looked about twenty-two, unmarried, fresh and hopeful – hope, that was the thing about her – and she carried a small suitcase, just the size for a weekend. He hovered near her for a few minutes, and she gave him not the slightest glance. She stood at the right of the big doors and inside them, stretching on tiptoe now and then to see over the rushing, bumping crowds. A glow of light from the doorway showed her rounded, pinkish cheek, the sheen of her hair, the eagerness of her straining eyes. It was already 6.35.

Of course, it might not be she, he thought. Then he felt suddenly bored, vaguely ashamed of himself, and walked over to Third Avenue to get something to eat, or at least a cup of coffee. He went into a coffee shop. He had bought a newspaper, and he propped it up and tried to read as he waited to be served. But when the waitress came, he realised he did not want anything, and got up with a murmured apology. He'd go back and see if the girl was still there, he thought. He hoped she wasn't there, because it was a rotten trick he'd played. If she was still there, he really ought to confess to her that it was a trick.

She was still there. As soon as he saw her, she started walking with her suitcase toward the information desk. He watched her circle the information desk and come back again, start for the same spot by the doors, then change it for the other side, as if for luck. And the beautiful, flying line of her eyebrow was tensely set now at an angle of tortured waiting, of almost hopeless hope.

But there is still that shred of hope, he thought to himself, and simple as it was, he felt it the strongest concept, the strongest truth that had ever come to him.

He walked past her, and now she did glance at him, and looked immediately beyond him. She was staring across Lexington Avenue and into space. Her young, round eyes were brightening with tears, he noticed.

With his hands in his pockets, he strolled past, looking her straight in the face, and as she glanced irritably at him, he smiled. Her eyes came back to him, full of shock and resentment, and he laughed, a short laugh that simply burst from him. But he might as well have cried, he thought. He just happened to have laughed instead. He knew what the girl was feeling. He knew exactly.

'I'm sorry,' he said.

She started, and looked at him in puzzled surprise.

'Sorry,' he repeated, and turned away.

When he looked back, she was staring at him with a frowning bewilderment that was almost like fear. Then she looked away and stretched superiorly high on her toes to peer over the bobbing heads – and the last thing he saw of her was her shining eyes with the determined, senseless, self-abandoned hope in them.

And as he walked up Lexington Avenue, he did cry. Now his eyes were exactly like those of the girl, he knew, shining, full of a relentless hope. He lifted his head proudly. He had his letter to Rosalind to write tonight. He began to compose it.

The Terrapin

Victor heard the elevator door open, his mother's quick footsteps in the hall, and he flipped his book shut. He shoved it under the sofa pillow out of sight, and winced as he heard it slip between sofa and wall to the floor with a thud. Her key was in the lock.

'Hello, Vee-ector-r!' she cried, raising one arm in the air. Her other arm circled a brown paper bag, her hand held a cluster of little bags. 'I have been to my publisher and to the market and also to the fish market,' she told him. 'Why aren't you out playing? It's a lovely, lovely day!'

'I was out,' he said. 'For a little while. I got cold.'

'Ugh!' She was unloading the grocery bag in the tiny kitchen off the foyer. 'You are seeck, you know that? In the month of October, you are cold? I see all kinds of children playing on the sidewalk. Even, I think, that boy you like. What's his name?'

'I don't know,' Victor said. His mother wasn't really listening anyway. He pushed his hands into the pockets of his short, too small shorts, making them tighter than ever, and walked aimlessly around the living-room, looking down at his heavy, scuffed shoes. At least his mother had to buy him shoes that fit him, and he rather liked these shoes, because they had the thickest soles of any he had ever owned, and they had heavy toes that rose up a little, like mountain climbers' shoes. Victor paused at the window and looked straight out at a toast-coloured apartment building across Third Avenue. He and his mother lived on the eighteenth floor, next to the top floor where the penthouses were. The building across the street was even taller than this one. Victor had liked their Riverside Drive apartment better. He had liked the school he had gone to there better. Here they laughed at his clothes. In the other school, they had finally got tired of laughing at them.

'You don't want to go out?' asked his mother, coming into the living-room, wiping her hands briskly on a paper bag. She sniffed her palms. 'Ugh! That stee-enk!'

'No, Mama,' Victor said patiently.

'Today is Saturday.'

'I know.'

'Can you say the days of the week?'

'Of course.'

'Say them.'

'I don't want to say them. I know them.' His eyes began to sting around the edges with tears. 'I've known them for years. Years and years. Kids five years old can say the days of the week.'

But his mother was not listening. She was bending over the drawing-table in the corner of the room. She had worked late on something last night. On his sofa bed in the opposite corner of the room, Victor had not been able to sleep until two in the morning, when his mother had gone to bed on the studio couch.

'Come here, Veector. Did you see this?'

Victor came on dragging feet, hands still in his pockets. No, he hadn't even glanced at her drawing-board this morning, hadn't wanted to.

'This is Pedro, the little donkey. I invented him last night. What do you think? And this is Miguel, the little Mexican boy who rides him. They ride and ride all over Mexico, and Miguel thinks they are lost, but Pedro knows the way home all the time, and ...'

Victor did not listen. He deliberately shut his ears in a way he had learned to do from many years of practice, but boredom, frustration – he knew the word frustration, had read all about it – clamped his shoulders, weighted like a stone in his body, pressed hatred and tears up to his eyes, as if a volcano were churning in him. He had hoped his mother might take a hint

35

from his saying that he was cold in his silly short shorts. He had hoped his mother might remember what he had told her, that the fellow he had wanted to get acquainted with downstairs, a fellow who looked about his own age, eleven, had laughed at his short pants on Monday afternoon. *They make you wear your kid brother's pants or something?* Victor had drifted away, mortified. What if the fellow knew he didn't even own any longer pants, not even a pair of knickers, much less *long* pants, even blue jeans! His mother, for some cock-eyed reason, wanted him to look 'French', and made him wear short shorts and stockings that came to just below his knees, and dopey shirts with round collars. His mother wanted him to stay about six years old, for ever, all his life. She liked to test out her drawings on him. *Veector is my sounding board,* she sometimes said to her friends. *I show my drawings to Veector and I know if children will like them.* Often Victor said he liked stories that he did not like, or drawings that he was indifferent to, because he felt sorry for his mother and because it put her in a better mood if he said he liked them. He was quite tired now of children's book illustrations, if he had ever in his life liked them – he really couldn't remember – and now he had two favourites: Howard Pyle's illustrations in some of Robert Louis Stevenson's books and Cruikshank's in Dickens. It was too bad, Victor thought, that he was absolutely the last person of whom his mother should have asked an opinion, because he simply *hated* children's illustrations. And it was a wonder his mother didn't see this, because she hadn't sold any illustrations for books for years and years, not since *Wimple-Dimple*, a book whose jacket was all torn and turning yellow now from age, which sat in the centre of the bookshelf in a little cleared spot, propped up against the back of the bookcase so everyone could see it. Victor had been seven years old when that book was printed. His mother liked to tell people and remind him, too, that he had told her what he had wanted to see her draw, had watched her make every drawing, had shown his opinion by laughing or not, and that she had been absolutely guided by him. Victor doubted this very much, because first of all the story was somebody else's and had been written before his mother did the drawings, and her drawings had had to follow the story, naturally. Since then, his mother had done only a few illustrations now and then for magazines for children, how to make paper pumpkins and black paper cats for Hallowe'en and things like that, though she took her portfolio around to publishers all the time. Their income came from his father, who was a wealthy businessman in France, an exporter of perfumes. His mother said he was very wealthy and very handsome. But he married again, he never wrote, and Victor had no interest in him, didn't even care if he never saw a picture of him, and he never had. His father was French with some Polish, and his mother was Hungarian with some French. The word Hungarian made Victor think of gypsies, but when he had asked his mother once, she had said emphatically that she hadn't any gypsy blood, and she had been annoyed that Victor brought the question up.

And now she was sounding him out again, poking him in the ribs to make him wake up, as she repeated:

'Listen to me! Which do you like better, Veector? "In all Mexico there was no bur-r-ro as wise as Miguel's Pedro," or "Miguel's Pedro was the wisest bur-r-ro in all Mexico."?'

'I think – I like it the first way better.'

'Which way is that?' demanded his mother, thumping her palm down on the illustration.

Victor tried to remember the wording, but realized he was only staring at the pencil smudges, the thumbprints on the edge of his mother's illustration board. The coloured drawing in the centre did not interest him at all. He was not-thinking. This was a frequent, familiar sensation to him now, there was something exciting and important about not-thinking, Victor felt, and he thought one day he would find something about it – perhaps under another name – in the Public Library or in the psychology books around the house that he browsed in when his mother was out.

'Veec-tor! What are you doing?'

'Nothing, Mama!'

'That is exactly it! Nothing! Can you not even *think*?'

A warm shame spread through him. It was as if his mother read his thoughts about not-thinking. 'I am thinking,' he protested. 'I'm thinking about *not*-thinking.' His tone was defiant. What could she do about it, after all?

'About what?' Her black, curly head tilted, her mascaraed eyes narrowed at him.

'Not-thinking.'

His mother put her jewelled hands on her hips. 'Do you know, Veec-tor, you are a little bit strange in the head?' She nodded. 'You are seeck. Psychologically seeck. And retarded, do you know that? You have the behaviour of a leetle boy five years old,' she said slowly and weightily. 'It is just as well you spend your Saturdays indoors. Who knows if you would not walk in front of a car, eh? But that is why I love you, little Veector.' She put her arm around his shoulders, pulled him against her and for an instant Victor's nose pressed into her large, soft bosom. She was wearing her flesh-coloured dress, the one you could see through a little where her breast stretched it out.

Victor jerked his head away in a confusion of emotions. He did not know if he wanted to laugh or cry.

His mother was laughing gaily, her head back. 'Seeck you are! Look at you! My lee-tle boy still, lee-tle short pants – Ha! Ha!'

Now the tears showed in his eyes, he supposed, and his mother acted as if she were enjoying it! Victor turned his head away so she would not see his eyes. Then suddenly he faced her. 'Do you think I like these pants? *You* like them, not me, so why do you have to make fun of them?'

'A lee-tle boy who's crying!' she went on, laughing.

Victor made a dash for the bathroom, then swerved away and dived on to the sofa, his face toward the pillows. He shut his eyes tight and opened his mouth, crying but not-crying in a way he had learned through practice also. With his mouth open, his throat tight, not breathing for nearly a minute, he could somehow get the satisfaction of crying, screaming even, without anybody knowing it. He pushed his nose, his open mouth, his teeth, against the tomato-red sofa pillow, and though his mother's voice went on in a lazily mocking tone, and her laughter went on, he imagined that it was getting fainter and more distant from him. He imagined, rigid in every muscle, that he was suffering the absolute worst that any human being could suffer. He imagined that he was dying. But he did not think of death as an escape, only as a concentrated and a painful incident. This was the climax of his not-crying. Then he breathed again, and his mother's voice intruded:

'Did you hear me? – *Did you hear me*? Mrs Badzerkian is coming for tea. I want you to wash your face and put on a clean shirt. I want you to recite something for her. Now what are you going to recite?'

'In winter when I go to bed,' said Victor. She was making him memorize every poem in *A Child's Garden of Verses*. He had said the first one that came into his head, and now there was an argument, because he had recited that one the last time. 'I said it, because I couldn't think of any other one right off the bat!' Victor shouted.

'Don't yell at me!' his mother cried, storming across the room at him.

She slapped his face before he knew what was happening.

He was up on one elbow on the sofa, on his back, his long, knobby-kneed legs splayed out in front of him. All right, he thought, if that's the way it is, that's the way it is. He looked at her with loathing. He would not show the slap had hurt, that it still stung. No more tears for today, he swore, no more even not-crying. He would finish the day, go through the tea, like a stone, like a soldier, not wincing. His mother paced around the room, turning one of her rings round and round, glancing at him from time to time, looking quickly away from him. But his eyes were steady on her. He was not afraid. She could even slap him again and he wouldn't care.

At last, she announced that she was going to wash her hair, and she went into the bathroom.

Victor got up from the sofa and wandered across the room. He wished he had a room of his own to go to. In the apartment on Riverside Drive, there had been three rooms, a living-room and his and his mother's rooms. When she was in the living-room, he had been able to go into his bedroom and vice versa, but here . . . They were going to tear down the old building they had lived in on Riverside Drive. It was not a pleasant thing for Victor to think about. Suddenly remembering the book that had fallen, he pulled out the sofa and reached for it. It was Menninger's *The Human Mind*, full of fascinating case histories of people. Victor put it back on the bookshelf between an astrology book and *How to Draw*. His mother did not like him to read psychology books, but Victor loved them, especially ones with case histories in them. The people in the case histories did what they wanted to do. They were natural. Nobody bossed them. At the local branch library, he spent hours browsing through the psychology shelves. They were in the adults' section, but the librarian did not mind his sitting at the tables there, because he was quiet.

Victor went into the kitchen and got a glass of water. As he was standing there drinking it, he heard a scratching noise coming from one of the paper bags on the counter. A mouse, he thought, but when he moved a couple of the bags, he didn't see any mouse. The scratching was coming from inside one of the bags. Gingerly, he opened the bag with his fingers, and waited for something to jump out. Looking in, he saw a white paper carton. He pulled it out slowly. Its bottom was damp. It opened like a pastry box. Victor jumped in surprise. It was a turtle on its back, a live turtle. It was wriggling its legs in the air, trying to turn over. Victor moistened his lips, and frowning with concentration, took the turtle by its sides with both hands, turned him over and let him down gently into the box again. The turtle drew in its feet then, and its head stretched up a little and it looked straight at him. Victor smiled. Why hadn't his mother told him she'd brought him a present? A live turtle. Victor's eyes glazed with anticipation as he thought of taking the turtle down, maybe with a leash around its neck, to show the fellow who'd laughed at his short pants. He might change his mind about being friends with him, if he found he owned a turtle.

'Hey, Mama! Mama!' Victor yelled at the bathroom door. 'You brought me a tur-rtle?'

'A what?' The water shut off.

'A turtle! In the kitchen!' Victor had been jumping up and down in the hall. He stopped.

His mother had hesitated, too. The water came on again, and she said in a shrill tone, 'C'est une terrapène! Pour un ragoût!'

Victor understood, and a small chill went over him because his mother had spoken in French. His mother addressed him in French when she was giving an order that had to be obeyed, or when she anticipated resistance from him. So the terrapin was for a stew. Victor nodded to himself with a stunned resignation, and went back to the kitchen. For a stew. Well, the terrapin was not long for this world, as they say. What did the terrapin like to eat? Lettuce? Raw bacon? Boiled potato? Victor peered into the refrigerator.

He held a piece of lettuce near the terrapin's horny mouth. The terrapin did not open its mouth, but it looked at him. Victor held the lettuce near the two little dots of its nostrils, but if the terrapin smelled it, it showed no interest. Victor looked under the sink and pulled out a large wash pan. He put two inches of water into it. Then he gently dumped the terrapin into the pan. The terrapin paddled for a few seconds, as if it had to swim, then finding that its stomach sat on the bottom of the pan, it stopped, and drew its feet in. Victor got down on his knees and studied the terrapin's face. Its upper lip overhung the lower, giving it a rather stubborn and unfriendly expression, but its eyes – they were bright and shining. Victor smiled when he looked hard at them.

'Okay, monsieur terrapène,' he said, 'just tell me what you'd like to eat and we'll get it for you! – Maybe some tuna?'

They had had tuna fish salad yesterday for dinner, and there was a small bowl of it left over. Victor got a little chunk of it in his fingers and presented it to the terrapin. The terrapin was not interested. Victor looked around the kitchen, wondering, then seeing the sunlight on the floor of the living-room, he picked up the pan and carried it to the living-room and set it down so the sunlight would fall on the terrapin's back. All turtles liked sunlight, Victor thought. He lay down on the floor on his side, propped up on an elbow. The terrapin stared at him for a moment, then very slowly and with an air of forethought and caution, put out its legs and advanced, found the circular boundary of the pan, and moved to the right, half its body out of the shallow water. It wanted out, and Victor took it in one hand, by the sides, and said:

'You can come out and have a little walk.'

He smiled as the terrapin started to disappear under the sofa. He caught it easily, because it moved so slowly. When he put it down on the carpet, it was quite still, as if it had withdrawn a little to think what it should do next, where it should go. It was a brownish green. Looking at it, Victor thought of river bottoms, of river water flowing. Or maybe oceans. Where did terrapins come from? He jumped up and went to the dictionary on the bookshelf. The dictionary had a picture of a terrapin, but it was a dull, black and white drawing, not so pretty as the live one. He learned nothing except that the name was of Algonquian origin, that the terrapin lived in fresh or brackish water, and that it was edible. Edible. Well, that was bad luck, Victor thought. But he was not going to eat any terrapène tonight. It would be all for his mother, that ragoût, and even if she slapped him and made him learn an extra two or three poems, he would not eat any terrapin tonight.

His mother came out of the bathroom. 'What are you doing there? – Veector?'

Victor put the dictionary back on the shelf. His mother had

seen the pan. 'I'm looking at the terrapin,' he said, then realized the terrapin had disappeared. He got down on hands and knees and looked under the sofa.

'Don't put him on the furniture. He makes spots,' said his mother. She was standing in the foyer, rubbing her hair vigorously with a towel.

Victor found the terrapin between the wastebasket and the wall. He put him back in the pan.

'Have you changed your shirt?' asked his mother.

Victor changed his shirt, and then at his mother's order sat down on the sofa with *A Child's Garden of Verses* and tackled another poem, a brand new one for Mrs Badzerkian. He learned two lines at a time, reading it aloud in a soft voice to himself, then repeating it, then putting two, four and six lines together, until he had the whole thing. He recited it to the terrapin. Then Victor asked his mother if he could play with the terrapin in the bathtub.

'No! And get your shirt all splashed?'

'I can put on my other shirt.'

'No! It's nearly four o'clock now. Get that pan out of the living-room!'

Victor carried the pan back to the kitchen. His mother took the terrapin quite fearlessly out of the pan, put it back into the white paper box, closed its lid, and stuck the box in the refrigerator. Victor jumped a little as the refrigerator door slammed. It would be awfully cold in there for the terrapin. But then, he supposed, fresh or brackish water was cold now and then, too.

'Veector, cut the lemon,' said his mother. She was preparing the big round tray with cups and saucers. The water was boiling in the kettle.

Mrs Badzerkian was prompt as usual, and his mother poured the tea as soon as she had deposited her coat and pocketbook on the foyer chair and sat down. Mrs Badzerkian smelled of cloves. She had a small, straight mouth and a thin moustache on her upper lip which fascinated Victor, as he had never seen one on a woman before, not one at such short range, anyway. He never had mentioned Mrs Badzerkian's moustache to his mother, knowing it was considered ugly, but in a strange way, her moustache was the thing he liked best about her. The rest of her was dull, uninteresting, and vaguely unfriendly. She always pretended to listen carefully to his poetry recitals, but he felt that she fidgeted, thought of other things while he spoke, and was glad when it was over. Today, Victor recited very well and without any hesitation, standing in the middle of the living-room floor and facing the two women, who were then having their second cups of tea.

'Très bien,' said his mother. 'Now you may have a cookie.'

Victor chose from the plate a small round cookie with a drop of orange goo in its centre. He kept his knees close together when he sat down. He always felt Mrs Badzerkian looked at his knees and with distaste. He often wished she would make some remark to his mother about his being old enough for long pants, but she never had, at least not within his hearing. Victor learned from his mother's conversation with Mrs Badzerkian that the Lorentzes were coming for dinner tomorrow evening. It was probably for them that the terrapin stew was going to be made. Victor was glad that he would have the terrapin one more day to play with. Tomorrow morning, he thought, he would ask his mother if he could take the terrapin down on the sidewalk for a while, either on a leash or in the paper box, if his mother insisted.

' – like a chi-ild!' his mother was saying, laughing, with a glance at him, and Mrs Badzerkian smiled shrewdly at him with her small, tight mouth.

Victor had been excused, and was sitting across the room with a book on the studio couch. His mother was telling Mrs Badzerkian how he had played with the terrapin. Victor frowned down at his book, pretending not to hear. His mother did not like him to open his mouth to her or her guests once he had been excused. But now she was calling him her 'lee-tle ba-aby Veec-tor ...'

He stood up with his finger in the place in his book. 'I don't see why it's childish to look at a terrapin!' he said, flushing with sudden anger. 'They are very interesting animals, they – '

His mother interrupted him with a laugh, but at once the laugh disappeared and she said sternly, 'Veector, I thought I had excused you. Isn't that correct?'

He hesitated, seeing in a flash the scene that was going to take place when Mrs Badzerkian had left. 'Yes, Mama. I'm sorry,' he said. Then he sat down and bent over his book again. Twenty minutes later, Mrs Badzerkian left. His mother scolded him for being rude, but it was not a five- or ten-minute scolding of the kind he had expected. It lasted hardly two minutes. She had forgotten to buy heavy cream, and she wanted Victor to go downstairs and get some. Victor put on his grey woollen jacket and went out. He always felt embarrassed and conspicuous in the jacket, because it came just a little bit below his short pants, and he looked as if he had nothing on underneath the coat.

Victor looked around for Frank on the sidewalk, but he didn't see him. He crossed Third Avenue and went to a delicatessen in the big building that he could see from the living-room window. On his way back, he saw Frank walking along the sidewalk, bouncing a ball. Now Victor went right up to him.

'Hey,' Victor said. 'I've got a terrapin upstairs.'

'A what?' Frank caught the ball and stopped.

'A terrapin. You know, like a turtle. I'll bring him down tomorrow morning and show you, if you're around. He's pretty big.'

'Yeah? – why don't you bring him down now?

'Because we're gonna eat now,' said Victor. 'See you.' He went into his building. He felt he had achieved something. Frank had looked really interested. Victor wished he could bring the terrapin down now, but his mother never liked him to go out after dark, and it was practically dark now.

When Victor got upstairs, his mother was still in the kitchen.

Eggs were boiling and she had put a big pot of water on a back burner. 'You took him out again!' Victor said, seeing the terrapin's box on the counter.

'Yes, I prepare the stew tonight,' said his mother. 'That is why I need the cream.'

Victor looked at her. 'You're going to – You have to kill it tonight?'

'Yes, my little one. Tonight.' She jiggled the pot of eggs.

'Mama, can I take him downstairs to show Frank?' Victor asked quickly. 'Just for five minutes, Mama. Frank's down there now.'

'Who is Frank?'

'He's that fellow you asked me about today. The blond fellow we always see. Please, Mama.'

His mother's black eyebrows frowned. 'Take the terrapène downstairs? Certainly not. Don't be absurd, my baby! The terrapène is not a toy!'

Victor tried to think of some other lever of persuasion. He had not removed his coat. 'You wanted me to get acquainted with Frank – '

'Yes. What has that got to do with a terrapin?'

The water on the back burner began to boil.

'You see, I promised him I'd – ' Victor watched his mother lift the terrapin from the box, and as she dropped it into the boiling water, his mouth fell open. *'Mama!'*

'What is this? What is this noise?'

Victor, open-mouthed, stared at the terrapin whose legs were now racing against the steep sides of the pot. The terrapin's mouth opened, its eyes looked directly at Victor for an instant, its head arched back in torture, the open mouth sank beneath the seething water – and that was the end. Victor blinked. It was dead. He came closer, saw the four legs and the tail stretched out in the water, its head. He looked at his mother.

She was drying her hands on a towel. She glanced at him, then said, 'Ugh!' She smelled her hands, then hung the towel back.

'Did you have to kill him like that?'

'How else? The same way you kill a lobster. Don't you know that? It doesn't hurt them.'

He stared at her. When she started to touch him, he stepped back. He thought of the terrapin's wide open mouth, and his eyes suddenly flooded with tears. Maybe the terrapin had been screaming and it hadn't been heard over the bubbling of the water. The terrapin had looked at him, wanting him to pull him out, and he hadn't moved to help him. His mother had tricked him, done it so fast, he couldn't save him. He stepped back again. 'No, don't touch me!'

His mother slapped his face, hard and quickly.

Victor set his jaw. Then he about-faced and went to the closet and threw his jacket on to a hanger and hung it up. He went into the living-room and fell down on the sofa. He was not crying now, but his mouth opened against the sofa pillow. Then he remembered the terrapin's mouth and he closed his lips. The terrapin had suffered, otherwise it would not have moved its legs fast to get out. Then he wept, soundlessly as the terrapin, his mouth open. He put both hands over his face, so as not to wet the sofa. After a long while, he got up. In the kitchen, his mother was humming, and every few minutes he heard her quick, firm steps as she went about her work. Victor had set his teeth again. He walked slowly to the kitchen doorway.

The terrapin was out on the wooden chopping board, and his mother, after a glance at him, still humming, took a knife and bore down on its blade, cutting off the terrapin's little nails. Victor half closed his eyes, but he watched steadily. The nails, with bits of skin attached to them, his mother scooped off the board into her palm and dumped into the garbage bag. Then she turned the terrapin on to its back and with the same sharp, pointed knife, she began to cut away the pale bottom shell. The terrapin's neck was bent sideways. Victor wanted to look away, but still he stared. Now the terrapin's insides were all exposed, red and white and greenish. Victor did not listen to what his mother was saying, about cooking terrapins in Europe, before he

47

was born. Her voice was gentle and soothing, not at all like what she was doing.

'All right, don't look at me like that!' she suddenly threw at him, stomping her foot. 'What's the matter with you? Are you crazy? Yes, I think so! You are seeck, you know that?'

Victor could not touch any of his supper, and his mother could not force him to, even though she shook him by the shoulders and threatened to slap him. They had creamed chipped beef on toast. Victor did not say a word. He felt very remote from his mother, even when she screamed right into his face. He felt very odd, the way he did sometimes when he was sick at his stomach, but he was not sick at his stomach. When they went to bed, he felt afraid of the dark. He saw the terrapin's face very large, its mouth open, its eyes wide and full of pain. Victor wished he could walk out the window and float, go anywhere he wanted to, disappear, yet be everywhere. He imagined his mother's hands on his shoulders, jerking him back, if he tried to step out the window. He hated his mother.

He got up and went quietly into the kitchen. The kitchen was absolutely dark, as there was no window, but he put his hand accurately on the knife rack and felt gently for the knife he wanted. He thought of the terrapin, in little pieces now, all mixed up in the sauce of cream and egg yolks and sherry in the pot in the refrigerator.

His mother's cry was not silent; it seemed to tear his ears off. His second blow was in her body, and then he stabbed her throat again. Only tiredness made him stop, and by then people were trying to bump the door in. Victor at last walked to the door, pulled the chain bolt back, and opened it for them.

He was taken to a large, old building full of nurses and doctors. Victor was very quiet and did everything he was asked to do, and answered the questions they put to him, but only those questions, and since they didn't ask him anything about a terrapin, he did not bring it up.

When the Fleet Was In at Mobile

With the bottle of chloroform in her hand, Geraldine stared at the man asleep on the back porch. She could hear the deep in, short out breaths whistling through the moustache, the way he breathed when he wasn't going to wake up till high noon. He'd been asleep since he came in at dawn, and she'd never known anything to wake him up in mid-morning when he'd been drinking all night, had she? Now was certainly the time.

She ran in her silk-stockinged feet to the rag drawer below the kitchen cabinets, tore a big rag from a worn-out towel, and then a smaller one. She folded the big rag to a square lump and on second thought wet it at the sink, and after some trouble because her hands had started shaking, tied it in front of her nose and mouth with the cloth belt of the dress she'd just ironed and laid out to wear. Then she got the claw hammer from the tool drawer in case she would need it, and went out on the back porch. She drew the straight chair close to the bed, sat down, and unstoppered the bottle and soaked the smaller rag. She held the rag over his chest for a few moments, then brought it slowly up toward his nose. Clark didn't move. But it must be doing something to him, she thought, she could smell it herself, sweet and sick like funeral flowers, like death itself.

Behind her, she heard the whine Red Dog always gave at the crest of a yawn, and his groan as he turned around and lay down in a cooler spot by the side of the house, and she thought: everybody thinks the chloroform is for Red Dog, and there he is out there sleeping, as alive as he's been in fourteen years.

Clark moved his head up and down as if he were agreeing with her, and her hand, her rigid body, followed his nose like a part of him, and a voice inside her screamed: *I wouldn't have dreamed of doing this if there were any other way, but he won't even let me out of the house!*

And she thought of Mrs Trelawney's nod of approval when she told her she was going to put Red Dog to sleep, because it wasn't safe for strangers to come around any more, Red Dog nipping at them with his one eyetooth.

She peered at the pulse in Clark's temple. It beat at the bottom of a wriggly green vein along his hairline that had always reminded her of a map of the Mississippi River. Then the rag bumped the end of Clark's nose, he turned his head aside, and still her hand followed the nose as if she couldn't have dragged it away if she'd wanted to, and perhaps she couldn't have. But the black eyelashes did not move at all, and she remembered how distinguished she'd once thought Clark looked with the hollows either side of his high thin forehead and the black hair like a wild bush above it, and the black moustache so big it was old-fashioned but suited Clark, like his old-fashioned tailor-made jackets and his square-toed boots.

She looked at the grey alarm clock that had been watching it all from the shelf – for about seven minutes now. How long did it take? She opened the bottle and poured more until it fell cool on to her palm, and held it back under the nose. The pulse still beat, but the breaths were shorter and fainter. Her arm ached so, she looked off through the porch screen and tried to think of something else. A rooster crowed out by the cow barn, like a new day a-dawning, she thought remembering a song; and she counted twenty ticks on the clock, one for each year old she was, and looked at it, and it was twelve minutes now, and when she looked again, the pulse was gone. But she mustn't be fooled by that, she thought, and looked harder at the hairs in his nostrils that didn't move and maybe wouldn't have anyway, but she couldn't hear anything. Then she stood up, and on second thought set the rag on the black moustache and left it there. She stared at the arm lying out on the sheet and the hand, a well-shaped hand, she'd always thought, for all its hairiness, with the gold band on the little finger that was his mother's wedding ring, he said, but the very left hand that had hit her many a time nevertheless, and she'd probably felt the ring, too. She stood there several seconds, not knowing why, then she hurried into the kitchen and whipped off her apron and her housedress.

She put on the flowery-printed summer dress she deliberately hadn't worn much with Clark, because it reminded her of the happiest days at Mobile, tossed the ruffled short sleeves into place with a familiar almost forgotten shake of her shoulders that made her feel practically her old self again, and with the dress still unfastened, ran on tiptoe out on the porch and saw the rag was still lying on his mouth. For good measure, she poured the rest of the bottle on the rag. And didn't the claw hammer look silly now? She took the hammer back to the drawer.

When she was all dressed except for make-up, she took the towel from her face, and propped the window of her room as wide as it would go. She stepped back from the dresser mirror, appraising herself anxiously, then stepped forward and put wide arcs of red on the bows of her upper lip, the way she liked it, dropped a cloud of powder on her nose and spread it quickly in all directions. Her cheeks were so curved now, she'd hardly have known herself, she thought, but she wasn't too plump, just right. She still had that combination everyone said was unique of come-hither plus the bloom of youth, and how many girls had that? How many girls could be proposed to by a minister's son, which was what had happened to her in Montgomery, and then have a life like she'd had in Mobile, the toast of the fleet? She laughed archly at herself in the mirror, though without making a sound – but who was there to hear her if she did laugh – and jogged her brown-blonde curls superfluously with her palms. She'd curled her hair with the iron this morning after Clark got in, and done as good as job as she'd ever done in her life, though all the while she'd known what she was going to do to Clark. And had she packed the curling iron?

She dragged her old black suitcase from behind the curtain under the sink, and found the curling iron right on top. She went back into the bedroom for her handbag. Her cigarettes. She ran to get the package of Lucky Strikes from beside the soap dish in the kitchen, and for a moment her spaced front teeth bit her underlip, the pencilled eyebrows lifted with a deploring quiver, as she gazed for the last time at the red rickrack she'd tacked around the shelf to beautify it, which had been completely lost on Clark, then she turned and went across the back porch and out.

Red Dog whined at her, and she dropped the suitcase and ran back into the house with his empty pan, got a hunk of stale cornbread from the breadbox and crumbled it, scraped skillet grease over it and with reckless extravagance the rest of the beef stew, too. Wouldn't Red Dog be surprised at such food at eleven in the morning? Red Dog was so surprised, he got on to his legs for it, wagging his old red tail that was as thin and full of jagged points as a rooster feather.

Hopping and dodging the puddles of red water, she ran daintily in her high-heeled grey lizard pumps down the rut of a road across west meadow. She felt happy as a lark this morning in her best shoes that weren't at all practical for travelling, she supposed, with their open toes and heels, but gave her such a lift! At the edge of the thicket, she turned and looked back at the farm. It wasn't the time of day she liked best. She liked just before sunset and just after sunrise, when the sun caught the tops of things and the level country was dotted with little bright green islands and the grazing cows had streaks of red along their straight backs. Red and green like a Christmas tree, she'd said fourteen months ago when she'd come here to live with Clark, the land always so cool and fresh as if a light shower had just stopped falling and the sun had come out. It'll be Christmas from now on, Clark, she had said, feeling like the end of a movie, and the teeth bit ruefully for another delicious moment of self-pity. Good-bye to the long brown house, the cow barn and the henhouse and the little privy!

The northbound bus wouldn't pass for nearly an hour, she knew, so she went on across the highway and into the other woods where there was a brook, and sat down and washed the red mud off her heels with a piece of Kleenex. The smoke from her cigarette was exactly the colour of the Spanish moss. It drifted upward as slow and unbroken as if she sat in a nice room somewhere talking. She sprang to her feet at the sound of a motor, but it was only a big gasoline truck coming up from New Orleans, and then she did hear the bus purring around the curve and she should have known the gasoline truck wasn't it, because her heart jumped now as if all the happiness in the world lay in the bus, and she was out in the road waving her arm before she knew it. The many, many times she'd watched the bus go by without being able to catch it!

And now she was climbing aboard, the floor rattling and swaying under her feet, northward.

'Where're you going, ma'am?' the driver asked.

She almost said Mobile, but she laughed and said, 'Birmingham,' instead, which was where her sister lived. 'But I'd like to go to Alistaire first.' Alistaire was just a little town in northern Louisiana where she'd stayed overnight once with her parents when she was a child, and she'd planned on stopping there for a couple of hours on her way to Birmingham. She paid with the 10-dollar bill she'd taken from Clark's pocket that morning. Besides that, she had nine dollars saved out of grocery money when Clark had used to let her go with the Trelawneys to Etienne Station

The bus was so crowded, there were three or four people standing, but when she walked up the aisle, a young man in blue overalls got right up and gave her his seat. 'Thank you, sir,' she said.

'You're welcome, ma'am,' the young man said, and stood in the aisle beside her.

The woman next to her had a little boy asleep in her lap. His head pressed roundly against Geraldine's thigh. In a moment, she thought, she would ask the woman a question about her child, she didn't know what as yet. Loosening the imitation sable furpiece around her neck – she'd just realized from the dark blue splotch under the arm of the young man that it was really quite hot today – Geraldine settled back to enjoy the ride. She smiled up at the young man and he smiled back, and she thought: how nice everybody is on the bus and they know by looking at her she's just as nice as they are. And what a relief it was, too, not to have Clark along, accusing her of wanting to sleep with the young man in blue overalls, just because she'd accepted his seat! She shook her head deploringly, felt a curl come undone over her ear, and casually tucked it back. And accusing her of flirting with Mr Trelawney, when everybody knew Mrs Trelawney was her best friend and always was along when they drove to town, which was the only time she ever saw him.

'*Women that sleep with ten men at a time never get pregnant!*' Clark's voice boomed out from the privy before he banged the door to, and fidgeting, Gerlaldine leaned toward the woman beside her and asked, 'Do you have many children?' and the woman gave her such a long, funny stare that Geraldine almost laughed out loud despite herself before the woman answered:

'Four. That's enough.'

Geraldine nodded, and glanced up at the young man standing beside her who shifted and smiled down at her, showing pink gums and big white teeth with one upper molar missing. Young and shy and lonely, Gerlaldine thought, almost as fine as the young sailors in Mobile, only not so handsome as most, but she edged away from him nevertheless, because the blue overalls seemed to be rubbing against her shoulder in a way she didn't like, or was she getting just as prudish as Clark? Oh yes, if they asked her any questions, she'd tell them what a prudish old maid Clark really was, not even fulfilling his marital duties, not that she cared, but she'd heard a lot of women suing for divorce just for that. Then accusing *her* of not being able to have children! Everyone in Etienne Parish knew Clark was strange. He'd served a jail sentence for swindling a business partner when he was young, and not so long ago people couldn't remember had been clapped in jail for preaching religion, but preaching like a maniac and nearly killing a man who had disagreed with him. Geraldine crossed her legs and pulled her skirt down.

The bus made her feel safe and powerful, as if she were in the centre of a mountain, or awake in the centre of a rather heavy, pleasant dream that would just keep on and on. She might stay on until her money gave out, then stop off and take a job somewhere. She'd go back to her own name, Geraldine Ann Lewis, plain and simple, and rent a little furnished apartment and potter around every evening cooking things, going to a movie maybe once a week and to church Sunday mornings, and be very cautious about making friends, especially men friends.

The little boy's head pressed harder against her thigh, the bus turned, and she saw they were approaching a town. She didn't know it, she thought excitedly, but she did. It was Dalton.

And if anyone cared to question her as to why she had done what she did, she thought as she made her way down the aisle, taking her suitcase with her, she would tell them the whole story, how Clark had told her he loved her and asked her to marry him and live with him in his house near Etienne Station, north of New Orleans, and how she had cooked and cleaned and been the best wife she knew, and how as the months went on she saw that Clark really hated her and had only married her to be able to pick on her and – she saw it clearly now – had deliberately chosen a wife from a place like the Star Hotel so he could hold it over her and make himself feel superior. She poked her straws through the hole in the top of the milk container.

'Hey, cain't you say *nothin'*, girl?' It was the young man in the blue overalls, grinning down at her, the sudden burr of his voice making her think first of a man who'd bent down to say something to her in a wheatfield once where she'd come with her father to watch the threshing, then of the sailors' voices in Mobile, and fear dropped like a needle through her before she could even wonder why she'd thought of that wheatfield she hadn't thought of since, and she turned away, leaving the 15 cents on the counter, not knowing if it was his or hers, replying, strangely breathless:

'I just can't talk just now!'

She'd been riding several minutes on the bus before she noticed the young man wasn't aboard. If he got himself a girl in Dalton, she hoped she'd be a nice girl. But maybe he was just going home to his folks, why should she even think he was going to a girl? She'd stop thinking things like that once she got far enough away from Clark. Clark wouldn't even let her ride to Etienne Station with the Trelawneys any more. She could let them know about the last time she'd gone with the Trelawneys, when Clark had been off somewhere for two days and there'd been no food in the house. He'd knocked the groceries out of her arms and slapped her face, back and forth, not saying a word, until she just collapsed on the groceries, crying as if her heart would break. And the scar from the belt buckle, she could show them that.

Without looking at it, she massaged the U-shaped scar on the back of her hand. Since she had got on the bus, her hands had never been still, the long backward-bending fingers clamping the soft palms symmetrically against the corners of her handbag, only to fly off to some other perch, as if she kept trying to pose them properly for a photograph. Her lizard pumps stood upright, side by side on the vibrating floor.

Alistaire was the next rest-stop. She didn't remember too much about the town except the name, or perhaps the town had changed a good deal in ten years, but the name was enough, and the fact she'd spent one of those happy, carefree nights in a tourist home with her family on one of their summer vacations. The sun was already down, so she decided to stay the night and get an early start tomorrow, as her father had used to say on their tours in the car. 'Where you reckon we'll sleep *to-*

night, papa?' she or her sister Gladys would ask him from the back seat, where the khaki blankets and the picnic lunch and probably a watermelon would be tied up and stowed away in such apple-pie order it was a pleasure just to crawl in the little space beside her sister. Her father'd say, 'Lord knows, sugar,' or maybe, 'Guess we'll make Aunt Doris' by tonight, Gerrie. Remember your Aunt Doris?' which was almost as exciting as a new tourist home, because like as not, she'd have forgotten her aunt's house since the year before. Wouldn't she like to forget Clark's house in a year's time, too, but the memory didn't work like that once you were grown, she knew. She remembered the Star Hotel only too well after fourteen months, every six-sided tile in the brown-and-white floor of the lobby that always smelled of disinfectant like a clinic; and the view from her room window of the lighted glass star that hung over the entrance.

Not far from the bus stop, she found a house with a roomers sign on the front lawn, and though the woman seemed a little suspicious at first because she didn't have a car and then because she didn't have a man with her – but what could be suspicious about *not* having a man? – she was soon in a clean, very tastefully furnished front room all to herself. Geraldine bathed in the bathroom down the hall, lifting the washrag so the water ran caressingly down her arms and legs, thinking – 'How long it's been since you've been my very own!'

She put on her nightgown and went right to bed, because she wanted to lie in the dark and think. No one would likely find Clark for three days, she thought. His cheeses were due at Etienne Station tomorrow, but they were used to his being a day late when he was on a bender. And since this was Thursday, the Trelawneys weren't likely to stop by until Saturday when they went to town, if then.

'I married you to help you, but the truth's not in you. You are the first entirely evil human soul I ever saw and it's my everlasting curse that I'm married to you!'

She spread her legs restlessly under the sheet, and brought

them together again like scissors. The crisp new sheet rattled about her with a sound like thunder. She pressed her fingertips harder into her thighs. Her mother in Montgomery would say, 'Well, you did finally fill out, didn't you, child?' Geraldine turned on her side and let a few tears roll out, over the bridge of her nose and into the pillowcase, because her mother had been dead almost a year now. The wind gave a sigh that blew the bottoms of the curtains out, held them reaching toward her for a moment, then twirled them like two capes. And she let a few more tears roll, thinking of her and Marianne's apartment in Mobile and of how young and happy they'd been together when the fleet was first in. Oh, she'd tell them all about Mobile, too, if they wanted to ask her, she hadn't a thing to be ashamed of. It was the country's lawmakers themselves and the police who made money out of it who ought to be ashamed.

She wouldn't tell them about Doug, though, because it hadn't been his fault. She'd say she came to the Star Hotel accidentally when she hadn't any other place to stay, which was true. She could see herself telling it to some solemn judge with grey hair, asking him to judge for himself what on earth else she could have done – right up to the moment she lay here now in a strange tourist home – and she could hear him assuring her she couldn't have done otherwise. She'd come to Mobile with her friend Marianne Hughes, from Montgomery, to take factory jobs after they'd finished high school, but they'd had to take jobs as waitresses until the factory jobs were open. She and Marianne had had a little apartment together, and she'd been able to send fifteen dollars a week home to her mother, and they hadn't been there any time before the fleet came in. Not even the fleet, just a couple of cruisers and a destroyer stopping for repairs, but the city was suddenly full of sailors and officers, everything going full tilt day and night, and Marianne used to wake her up every morning at a quarter to six yelling, '*Out of bed, honey child, the fleet's in at Mobile!*' which might sound silly now she was grown, but at eighteen and free as the wind, it had made her jump out of bed feeling like a million dollars, laughing and tingling with energy, no matter how tired she might be really.

She and Marianne would throw on their waitress uniforms and hurry down to the restaurant without even coffee, through the streets that would be even then full of sailors, some up early and some still out and maybe drunk, but by and large, she'd still say they were the finest, cleanest young men she'd ever met. There were always sailors in the restaurant for breakfast, and she and Marianne would tell them they were going to work in the marine supplies factory in five weeks, and the sailors would probably ask them for dates, and if they were especially nice looking, she and Marianne would accept.

Then Marianne married a chief petty officer, and she'd had to give up the apartment. She'd known Douglas Ellison, a pharmacist's mate from Connecticut, for about three weeks then, and they intended to marry, too, when they were absolutely sure they loved each other. She hadn't yet found an apartment, so Doug had got her a room at the Star Hotel and paid a week's rent for it. And he stayed with her a couple of nights – the first fellow she'd ever had anything to do with, despite what most girls in Mobile were doing, Marianne included. His ship had been leaving at the end of the week, but he was due back in a month, and then they were going to be married.

That was also the month the job was to have been open at the factory, but wasn't. And then – it never rains but it pours – she lost her job at the restaurant, because the girl who'd had it before came back, or so they said, from the marine supplies factory that was laying off instead of hiring. And suddenly there were so many people unemployed, one couldn't even get a job washing dishes in exchange for three meals.

She'd been ready to go back to Montgomery, when the Star Hotel told her they couldn't get her trunk out of the basement for several more days, and upped the bill twice what it should have been so she wouldn't be able to pay it, and when she threatened to call the police, told her if she did, they'd have her in jail. She'd gone out to tell the police anyway, and the doorman had stopped her. Didn't she know the Star Hotel was a house, he said. Oh, she'd known a lot was going on at the Star Hotel, what else could you expect with the fleet in and right on the waterfront, but she hadn't known it was a common brothel. And suddenly there were strangers standing all around her, pretending to take it for granted she was one of those women, too, laughing at her when she said Doug Ellison was her fiancé. They dared her to talk to a policeman, the police would have her in for ten years, they said, and she got terrified. Some of the other girls there said they'd been in the same boat, but didn't mind now, because what work was there to be found outside anyway, and it was easier than a lot of work, whereupon she lost the bit of dinner she'd just eaten. She couldn't eat and barely slept, and they started sending sailors into her room as if she'd have anything to do with them after Doug Ellison. But no letter ever came from Doug, she knew because Connie, one of the girls there, promised she would see she got it, if it came. They watched the girls' mail, especially the outgoing, and she had to keep writing to her mother that she was still working at Carter's Restaurant and very happy, hoping her mother would read between the lines, but her mother's cancer was getting worse then, and she never did. The sailors that came into the Star Hotel, even if they were fairly decent looking, made her sick that she'd ever felt gay hearing Marianne yell in the mornings, and sicker that she'd ever thought she'd tell her grandchildren of the most exciting period in her life, stories that began, 'When the fleet was in at Mobile, I was just eighteen . . .'

And if anyone chose to cast the first stone at her because she finally yielded, she would relate how they stopped putting enough food on her trays, and how all the girls, even Connie Stegman, advised her to co-operate and lay a little money by, because they didn't give a snap for her life itself. But when they found she was hoarding her money, they came and found it and took it, for the truth was they didn't trust their own doorman when it came to taking bribes. She threatened to kill herself, and she meant it, so they sent her to Chattanooga with two other girls in a car, to a hotel owned by a partner of the Star Hotel manager. If anybody didn't believe her, let them go to Chattanooga and see the Blackstone Hotel standing there for themselves. Let them go inside and look around. She got so run down at the Blackstone, they sent her back to the Star Hotel. It worked this way: there was a whole syndicate all over the South, and wherever business was heavy, they shipped girls, or if they thought a girl was about to make a break, they shipped her where she didn't know anyone.

Geraldine sat up at the knock on the door.

'Got everything you need?' called the frail, high voice of the landlady.

'Yes – ' She swallowed air, and her heart beat wildly. 'Thank you.'

'There's ice water in the pitcher on the dresser. Hope you weren't asleep, didn't see no light.'

'No, I wasn't asleep,' said Geraldine, beginning to smile.

'Awful early,' said the woman pleasantly, sounding as if she were turning away.

'Yes, it is.' Geraldine wished she could think of something nicer to say. 'Good night,' she called, and lay down on her back, still smiling.

And then Clark. She'd tell them about those first four visits of Clark's to the Star Hotel and every word he said, and just let them judge for themselves. She could still see him exactly as he looked when he stepped into her room for the first time, a really impressive man with his straight back and heavy black brows and moustache. He'd had on his square-toed boots with his trouser cuffs tucked into them and his long, nearly black jacket, and she'd thought right away he looked like some kind of a statesman or maybe an actor around the time of the Civil War. He was still and formal and hardly said a word or even looked at her until just as he went out the door, and she remembered that look like no other, because it had scared her. If she had only obeyed her instinct then! He had turned with his hand on the knob of the open door and looked back at her over his shoulder, as if he might have forgotten something or as if he wanted to remember her because he hated her. She hadn't liked him at all, and when he came in a few days later, she'd been about to tell him to leave, when he just sat down and lighted a cigar and started talking. He wanted to know all about her, how old she was and how she happened to be there, and though his brown eyes were really quite kind, almost fatherly if it wasn't sacrilegious to say such a thing, she'd resented his idle curiosity and not answered much.

Then the third time, he had brought her candy, and the fourth time flowers, presenting them with a bow, and the fourth time she'd told him the whole story and cried on his shoulder when he sat down beside her, because she'd never told anyone, not even Connie Stegman, that much. 'What would you say if I asked you to be my wife?' he'd asked right out of the blue. 'You think it over till I come back. I'll be back in a week.' She hadn't believed him, but naturally she'd thought about it, about the farm he'd described in the flat country north of New Orleans, and the fancy cheeses he made for a living and the duck-callers he made out of wood and shipped to hunters everywhere — little wooden boxes with a cover that scraped and made a sound like a duck, he'd brought her one to show her — and she'd thought what a special kind of farmer he was, not just a dirt farmer but an educated gentleman. And the girls at the hotel told her how lucky she was, for Clark Reeder was a fine man even if he was over forty and a little old-fashioned, and Margaret the hotel director had told her how many girls had found themselves good husbands that way and how often the husbands came back and said what fine wives the girls made. So she'd thought about being mistress of a farmhouse that she would make neat as a pin and stock with good things to eat, but mainly of course she'd thought of being free and the next time he'd come, she'd said yes. And like a bird out of a cage, she'd almost died of happiness at first, not even wanting the honeymoon Clark had suggested, just wanting to get settled at home. She'd cooked and sewed and scrubbed every inch of the place and been delighted to do it. But why even tell them all that if they couldn't imagine it? Or how good it felt just to be treated like a human being again, the way Clark had said, 'Herbert,' speaking to Mr Trelawney, 'I'd like you to meet my wife,' presenting her on his hand as if she were a queen.

She was pumping water by the back steps and the pump was acting queer, making a boom-crash-boom whenever the water gushed out, spilling all over the bucket but not filling it, and even Red Dog was up looking at it. Then she opened her eyes and discovered the sound came from out the window – a military band! Either a parade or a circus, she thought, jumping out of bed as gaily as when Marianne used to awaken her. The music was coming from a park a couple of blocks down the street where she saw a lot of coloured lights like a celebration. She whirled around and pulled her nightgown over her head.

Clark!

He'd still be lying on the back porch with the rag on his moustache, if the breeze hadn't blown it off. She shimmied into her girdle. Well, so be it. Some actions were a necessity, like killing animals for food, or sawing through the bars of a prison to get free. And Clark's house had been a prison as bad as the Star Hotel, except he never touched her, saying she was too dirty for him. Clark set himself up as her saviour while telling her all the time she tortured him. Did it make any sense to torture her and torture himself, too? She made the two red arcs on her upper lip that Clark said made her look like a harlot but were simply better for her kind of mouth, and combed what was left of the curls into a loose short bob. She snatched up her handbag and went out into the hall, but on second thought came back and left her money except for one dollar in the pocket of her coat in the closet.

From the sidewalk she could see a striped tent top and something like a ferris wheel lighted up and spinning, and could hear a man yelling over a loud-speaker, and between the *boom-crash-booms* that were louder than anything, the band played a song she was pleased she could recognize as 'The Stars and Stripes For Ever'. She looked down and concentrated on getting across the dark road in her wobbly high heels. Her heart was going like sixty and she really must stop and get her breath before she went one step farther. And it was only a church benefit at that, she saw by the streamer over the entrance. FIRST METHODIST WELFARE NIGHT.

'*Admission only twenty-five cents!*' roared the voice on one note. '*And dig down in your pocket for a second quarter if you're really thinking of entering the Kingdom of Heaven!*'

Geraldine pushed her money through the high window. 'I'll pay my two quarters.'

'*One?*' a voice roared.

'One.'

The music stopped as soon as she went in, and there wasn't any band, she saw, it was all from the merry-go-round that had a drum and cymbal machine in the centre that kept going. A final *boom-crash* shimmered into silence, and Geraldine stood staring at the still bounding horses on the platform that made a hollow sound like roller skates on a wooden rink and for some reason excited her terribly. The roof of the merry-go-round was like a king's crown with gilt scallops hanging around the edge, each set with a blue or red light like a jewel. Suddenly something made her gasp, something blurred her vision with tears: she had been on this very spot before, been on this merry-go-round as a child, the time she'd passed through this town with her family. They might have stopped at the same tourist home for that matter. There was the Ferris wheel way back under the trees and the parking lot with the kerb around it where her father's big car had stood, and the separate booth that sold pink cotton candy, and the big ice-cream parlour with an open porch all around it like a summerhouse – all just as it had been one night so long ago she didn't really remember. And laughing at herself, she hurried to buy her merry-go-round ticket.

The glare of white lights made her feel positively naked as she stepped on to the platform, but there were so many other grown-up people getting on – maybe some like her, coming back after many years – she forgot her self-consciousness and weaved right through the maze of nickel-plated poles to the pink horse she wanted. The *boom-crash-boom* started with a terrible din right in her ears, then music so loud she couldn't recognize it and had to laugh, and the pink horse rose slowly up and down. She felt herself sink again, and closed her eyes, letting it catch her up in swifter and swifter rhythm, pulling her outward so she had to hold on with both hands. She felt so happy, she could have cried. What was it, she wondered, with the music pounding in your ears and your two hands holding the pole and the small rise, small fall, so wonderful beyond all . . . Her throat closed, and she opened her eyes, seeing a blur of black trees and sliding dots of lights and a few figures standing at the edge of darkness smiling up. Where were her parents? She wanted to wave to them. Then her shoulders crumpled as if she had been struck and the tears fairly leapt from her eyes, because she knew it was only to be a child, with her parents waving and shouting to her to hold on, only to be astride the horse in a short dress and to be put to bed in less than an hour and to be too small to reach the bottom of the bed with her toes, and to get up tomorrow to ride in the back of the car, asking, 'Where you reckon we'll sleep *tonight*, papa?' that was so wonderful, and it was all, all gone now for ever. She felt her face twist with a tragedy too profound for tears, and deliberately she looked away from the people standing watching to the merry-go-round's centre where the scenic pictures showed 'A Swiss Chalet', 'Pike's Peak', 'Venice', thinking quickly how she would tell them, if they asked her anything, how Clark had accused her of ever more disgusting practices, the worst he could think of, and how he brought men into the house on pretexts, just so he could accuse her of something later.

'Are you all right?' the man on the horse next to her asked, and realizing she'd been staring in his direction with what was probably a pretty funny expression, Geraldine said with a quick smile:

'Oh, perfectly all right, thank you.'

She put her head up then, her eyes darting to look at this and that as if she'd never been so gay in her life. A young man in a grey suit was waving at her from the other side of the merry-go-round, and she almost waved back, thinking she must know him, but she didn't. Or maybe he wasn't even waving at her, but she saw now he was, and she did know him, too. He was a boy she'd known in high school in Montgomery! His name was Franky McSomething, she remembered.

Now he waved at her again, and she gave a little wave back, timid as if she were merely brushing something out of the air in front of her, and when he smiled wider, she saw the two creases down his lean cheeks and the bright brown eyes not slipping away shyly as they used to do, but looking right back at her. Hadn't Franky grown up! He clearly wanted to talk to her, and maybe they'd have a soda in the ice-cream parlour and get re-acquainted and maybe like a fairytale Franky would fall in love with her again. He'd had a crush on her one term, but he'd been such a bashful, watching-from-a-distance sort of boy, nothing had happened. Well, she knew how to put men at their ease now.

She watched Franky dismount as the horses slowed, and noticed how tall he'd grown and how clean-cut he looked with his collar and tie. She slipped down from her own horse. The platform was making the hollow sound of the roller-skating rink, but slower and slower, and there was a strange moment when she felt suddenly as sad and melancholy as autumn, really as sad as she'd ever felt in her life, so she had to force herself to smile as she stepped down to meet Franky who was holding his hand out for hers.

'Is your name Ger – Geraldine?' he asked, making her laugh, because he was still as bashful as ever after all.

'Yes, and you're – Franky?'

He nodded with a smile and led her gently away. 'Yes.'

'Well, how are things back in Montgomery?' she asked.

'Oh, they're all right. What've you been doing?'

'Well, I had a job in Mobile for a while. I was in Mobile th(

time the fleet was in, we always said, but it wasn't the fleet, just a couple of cruisers and a destroyer stopping for repairs, but it was mighty gay!' She tipped her head back and swung her hand that Franky was holding. Franky had a little scar now on the bridge of his nose, and she thought of the scar on the back of her hand and decided not to ask him about his. Life had left its marks on both of them, she supposed, though they were still so young.

'Cigarette?'

'Still as shy as ever, Franky?' she blurted, because she thought his hand shook as he lighted it for her, though her hand was shaking, too.

Franky smiled. 'How about a cold drink, Geraldine?'

'Why, I'd love one!'

They stepped up on the open porch of the ice-cream parlour and sat down at one of the tables. Franky stared shyly past her, and she thought he nodded to someone and looked behind her, but it was only the waiter coming. They ordered black and white sodas.

'Are you living here now?' Franky asked her.

'No-o, just passing through. But I like it so here,' she hurried to add, 'I just might live here. Do you know I realized after I'd came here tonight that I'd been to this park before when I was a little girl? Oh, long before I even knew you!' She laughed. 'Are you living here now?'

'Um-hm,' he replied, still looking so pained and stiff that Geraldine had to smile.

She said nothing, letting her eyes roll up at the honeysuckle that grew along the porch eaves.

'You were in –'

'What?' Geraldine prompted.

'You were in a little town above New Orleans, weren't you, Geraldine?'

He'd even taken the trouble to ask her mother about her! 'Why, yes,' she said. She glanced up at a man in a dark suit standing by her elbow. There was another man on her right,

67

between her and the porch rail. She looked at Franky with a bewildered smile.

Franky said, 'These are my friends, Geraldine. You'll come with us, won't you?' He stood up.

'But I didn't finish my –' The man on her left took her arm. She looked at Franky and saw his mouth close in a straight line she didn't know at all. The other man took her other arm. Franky wasn't making a move to help her, wasn't even looking! 'You're not – you're not Franky!'

Franky pulled something from his inside coat pocket and held it toward her.

LOUISIANA STATE POLICE, Geraldine read on a card in the billfold. She wanted to scream, but her mouth only hung open, limp.

The man who looked like Franky stood there staring at her, pocketing his billfold. 'It's all right,' he said so softly she could hardly hear. 'Your husband isn't dead. He just asked us to find you.'

Then her scream came as if it had been waiting just for that. She heard it reach the farthest corners of the park, and though they yanked her with them around the table, she took another breath and let it go again, let it shatter all the leaves and shatter her body, while she stared at the man in the grey suit simply because he wasn't Franky. Then his face and the lights and the park went out, though she knew as well as she knew she still screamed that her eyes were open under her hands.

The Quest for *Blank Claveringi*

Avery Clavering, a professor of zoology at a California university, heard of the giant snails of Kuwa in a footnote of a book on molluscs. His sabbatical had been coming up in three months when he read the few lines:

It is said by Matusas Islands natives that snails even larger than this exist on the uninhabited island of Kuwa, twenty-five miles distant from the Matusas. The Matusans claim that these snails have a shell diameter of twenty feet and that they are man-eating. Dr Wm J. Stead, now living in the Matusas, visited Kuwa in 1949 without finding any snails at all, but the legend persists.

The item aroused Professor Clavering's interest, because he very much wanted to discover some animal, bird, reptile or even mollusc to which he could give his name. *Something-or-other Claveringi*. The professor was forty-eight. His time, perhaps, was not growing short, but he had achieved no particular renown. The discovery of a new species would win him immortality in his field.

The Matusas, the professor saw on a map, were three small islands arranged like the points of an isosceles triangle not far from Hawaii. He wrote a letter to Dr Stead and received the following reply, written on an abominable typewriter, so many words pale, he could scarcely read it:

April 8th, 19 –

Dear Professor Clavering:
I have long heard of the gaint snails of Kuwa, but before you make a trip of such length, I must tell you that the natives here assure me a group of them went about twenty years ago to Kuwa to exterminate these so-called man-eating snails which they imagined could swim the

ocean between Kuwa and the Matusas and do some damage to the
latter island. They claim to have killed off the whole community of
them except for one old fellow they could not kill. This is typical of
native stories – there's always one that got away. I haven't much
doubt the snails were not bigger than three feet across and that they
were not **** (here a word was illegible, due both to the pale ribbon
and a squashed insect). You say you read of my effort in 1949 to find
the giant snails. What the footnote did not say is that I have made
several trips since to find them. I retired to the Matusas, in fact, for
that purpose. I now believe the snails to be mere folklore, a figment
of the natives' imagination. If I were you, I would not waste time or
money on an expedition.

> Yours sincerely,
> Wm J. Stead, M.D.

Professor Clavering had the money and the time. He detected
a sourness in Dr Stead's letter. Maybe Dr Stead had just had bad
luck. By post, Professor Clavering hired a thirty-foot sail-boat
with an auxiliary motor from Hawaii. He wanted to make the
trip alone from the Matusas. *Blank Claveringi.* Regardless of the
size, the snail was apt to be different from any known snail,
because of its isolation – if it existed. He planned to go one
month ahead of his wife and to join her and their twenty-year-
old daughter Wanda in Hawaii for a more orthodox holiday
after he had visited Kuwa. A month would give him plenty
of time to find the snail, even if there were only one, to take
photographs, and make notes.

It was late June when Professor Clavering, equipped with
water tanks, tinned beef, soup and milk, biscuits, writing
materials, camera, knife, hatchet and a Winchester .22 which
he hardly knew how to use, set forth from one of the Matusas
bound for Kuwa. Dr Stead, who had been his host for a few days,
saw him off. Dr Stead was seventy-five, he said, but he looked
older, due perhaps to the ravages of drink and the apparently
aimless life he led now. He had not looked for the giant snail in
two years, he said.

'I've given the last third of my life to looking for this snail, you might say,' Dr Stead added 'But that's man's fate, I suppose, the pursuit of the non-existent. Well – good luck to you, Professor Clavering!' He waved his old American straw hat as the *Samantha* left the dock under motor power.

Professor Clavering had made out to Stead that if he did find snails, he would come back at once, get some natives to accompany him, and return to Kuwa with materials to make crates for the snails. Stead had expressed doubt whether he could persuade any natives to accompany him, if the snail or snails were really large. But then, Dr Stead had been negative about everything pertaining to Professor Clavering's quest. Professor Clavering was glad to get away from him.

After about an hour, Professor Clavering cut the motor and tentatively hoisted some sail. The wind was favourable, but he knew little about sails, and he paid close attention to his compass. At last, Kuwa came into view, a tan hump on a sea of blue. He was quite close before he saw any greenery, and this was only the tops of some trees. Already, he was looking for anything resembling a giant snail, and regretting he had not brought binoculars, but the island was only three miles long and one mile broad. He decided to aim for a small beach. He dropped anchor, two of them, in water so clear he could see the sand under it. He stood for a few minutes on the deck.

The only life he saw was a few birds in the tops of trees, brightly coloured, crested birds, making cries he had never heard before. There was no low-lying vegetation whatsoever, none of the grass and reeds that might have been expected on an island such as this – much like the Matusas in the soil colour – and this augured well of the presence of snails that might have devoured everything green within their reach. It was only a quarter to two. Professor Clavering ate part of a papaya, two boiled eggs, and brewed coffee on his alcohol burner, as he had had nothing to eat since 6 a.m. Then with his hunting knife and hatchet in the belt of his khaki shorts, and his camera around his neck, he lowered himself into the water. The *Samantha* carried no rowboat.

He sank up to his neck, but he could walk on the bottom. He held the camera high. He emerged panting, as he was some twenty pounds overweight. Professor Clavering was to regret every one of those pounds before the day was over, but as he got his breath and looked around him, and felt himself drying off in the warm sunlight, he was happy. He wiped his hatchet and knife with dry sand, then walked inland, alert for the rounded form of a snail's shell, moving or stationary, anywhere. But as snails were more or less nocturnal, he thought any snails might well be sleeping in some cave or crevice with no idea of emerging until nightfall.

He decided to cross the island first, then follow the coast to right or left and circle the island. He had not gone a quarter of a mile, when his heart gave a leap. Ten yards before him, he saw three bent saplings with their top leaves chewed off. The young trees were four inches in diameter at their base. It would have taken a considerable weight to bend them down, something like a hundred pounds. The professor looked on the trees and the ground for the glaze left by snails, but found none. But rain could have washed it away. A snail whose shell was three feet in diameter would not weigh enough to bend such a tree, so Professor Clavering now hoped for something bigger. He pushed on.

He arrived at the other side of the island. The sea had eaten a notch into the shore, forming a mostly dry gully of a hundred yards' length and a depth of thirty feet. The land here was sandy but moist, and there was, he saw, a little vegetation in the form of patchy grass. But here, the lower branches of all the trees had been divested of their leaves, and so long ago that the branches had dried and fallen off. All this bespoke the presence of land snails. Professor Clavering stooped and looked down into the gulley. He saw, just over the edge of his side of the crevice, the pink-tan curve of something that was neither rock nor sand. If it was a snail, it was monstrous. Involuntarily, he took a step backward, scattering pebbles down the gulley.

The professor ran round the gulley to have a better look. It was a snail, and its shell was about fifteen feet high. He had a view of its left side, the side without the spiral. It resembled a peach-coloured sail filled with wind, and the sunlight made nacreous, silvery patches gleam and twinkle as the great thing stirred. The little rain of pebbles had aroused it, the professor realized. If the shell was fifteen or eighteen feet in diameter, he reckoned that the snail's body or foot would be something like six yards long when extended. Rooted to the spot, the professor stood, thrilled as much by the (as yet) empty phrase *Blank Claveringi* which throbbed in his head as by the fact he was looking upon something no man had seen before, or at least no scientist. The crate would have to be bigger than he had thought, but the *Samantha* would be capable of taking it on her forward deck.

The snail was backing to pull its head from the narrow part of the gulley. The moist body, the color of tea with milk, came into view with the slowness of an enormous snake awakening from slumber. All was silent, except for pebbles dropping from the snail's underside as it lifted its head, except for the professor's constrained breathing. The snail's head, facing inland, rose higher and higher, and its antennae, with which it saw, began to extend. Professor Clavering realized he had disturbed it from its diurnal sleep, and a brief terror caused him to retreat again, sending more pebbles down the slope.

The snail heard this, and slowly turned its enormous head toward him.

The professor felt paralysed. A gigantic face regarded him, a face with drooping, scalloped cheeks or lips, with antennae six feet long now, the eyes on the ends of them scrutinizing him at his own level and scarcely ten feet away, with the disdain of a Herculean lorgnette, with the unknown potency of a pair of over-sized telescopes. The snail reared so high, it had to arch its antennae to keep him in view. Six yards long? It would be more like eight or ten yards. The snail turned itself to move toward him.

Still, the professor did not budge. He knew about snails'

teeth, the twenty-odd thousand pairs of them even in a small garden snail, set in comblike structures, the upper front teeth visible, moving up and down constantly just under transparent flesh. A snail of this size, with proportionate teeth, could chew through a tree as quickly as a woodsman's axe, the professor thought. The snail was advancing up the bank with monumental confidence. He had to stand still for a few seconds simply to admire it. *His* snail! The professor opened his camera and took a picture, just as the snail was hauling its shell over the edge of the quarry.

'You are magnificent!' Professor Clavering said in a soft and awestruck voice. Then he took a few steps backward.

It was pleasant to think he could skip nimbly about, comparatively speaking, observing the snail from all angles, while the snail could only creep toward him at what seemed the rate of one yard in ten seconds. The professor thought to watch the snail for an hour or so, then go back to the *Samantha* and write some notes. He would sleep aboard the boat, take some more photographs tomorrow morning, then start under engine power back to the Matusas. He trotted for twenty yards, then turned to watch the snail approach.

The snail travelled with its head lifted three feet above the ground, keeping the professor in the focus of its eyes. It was moving faster. Professor Clavering retreated sooner than he intended, and before he could get another picture.

Now Professor Clavering looked around for a mate of the snail. He was rather glad not to see another snail, but he cautioned himself not to rule out the possibility of a mate. It wouldn't be pleasant to be cornered by two snails, yet the idea excited him. Impossible to think of a situation in which he could not escape from two slow, lumbering creatures like the — the what? *Amygdalus Persica* (his mind stuck on peaches, because of the beautiful colour of the shell) *Carnivora* (perhaps) *Claveringi*. That could be improved upon, the professor thought as he walked backward, watching.

A little grove of trees gave him an idea. If he stood in the grove, the snail could not reach him, and he would also have a close view. The professor took a stand amid twelve or fifteen trees, all about twenty feet high. The snail did not slacken its speed, but began to circle the grove, still watching the professor. Finding no opening big enough between two trees, the snail raised its head higher, fifteen feet high, and began to creep up on the trees. Branches cracked, and one tree snapped.

Professor Clavering ducked and retreated. He had a glimpse of a great belly gliding unhurt over a jagged tree trunk, of a circular mouth two feet across, open and showing the still wider upper band of teeth like shark's teeth, munching automatically up and down. The snail cruised gently down over the tree tops, some of which sprang back into position as the snail's weight left them.

Click! went the professor's camera.

What a sight that had been! Something like a slow hurdle. He imagined entertaining friends with an account of it, substantiated by the photograph, once he got back to California. Old Professor McIlroy of the biology department had laughed at him for spending seven thousand dollars on an effort he predicted would be futile!

Professor Clavering was tiring, so he cut directly for the *Samantha*. He noticed that the snail veered also in a direction that would intercept him, if they kept on at their steady though different speeds, and the professor chuckled and trotted for a bit. The snail also picked up speed, and the professor remembered the wide, upward rippling of the snail's body as it had hurdled the trees. It would be interesting to see how fast the snail could go on a straight course. Such a test would have to wait for America.

He reached the water and saw his beach a few yards away to his right, but no ship was there. He'd made a mistake, he thought, and his beach was on the other side of the island. Then he caught sight of the *Samantha* half a mile out on the ocean, drifting away.

'*Damn!*' Professor Clavering said aloud. He'd done something wrong with the anchors. Did he dare try to swim to it? The distance frightened him, and it was growing wider every moment.

A rattle of pebbles behind him made him turn. The snail was hardly twenty feet away.

The professor trotted down toward the beach. There was bound to be some slit on the coast, a cave however small, where he could be out of reach of the snail. He wanted to rest for a while. What really annoyed him now was the prospect of a chilly night without blankets or food. The Matusas natives had been right: there was nothing to eat on Kuwa.

Professor Clavering stopped dead, his shoes sliding on sand and pebbles. Before him, not fifty feet away on the beach, was another snail as big as the one following him, and somewhat lighter in colour. Its tail was in the sea, and its muzzle dripped water as it reared itself to get a look at him.

It was this snail, the professor realized, that had chewed through the hemp ropes and let the boat go free. Was there something about new hemp ropes that appealed to snails? This question he put out of his mind for the nonce. He had a snail before and behind him. The professor trotted on along the shore. The only crevice of shelter he was sure existed was the gulley on the other side of the island. He forced himself to walk at a moderate pace for a while, to breathe normally, then he sat down and treated himself to a rest.

The first snail was the first to appear, and as it had lost sight of him, it lifted its head and looked slowly to right and left, though without slackening its progress. The professor sat motionless, bare head lowered, hoping the snail would not see him. But he was not that lucky. The snail saw him and altered course to a straight line for him. Behind it came the second snail – it's wife? its husband? – the professor could not tell and there was no way of telling.

Professor Clavering had to leave his resting place. The weight of his hatchet reminded him that he at least had a weapon. A good scare, he thought, a minor wound might discourage them.

He knew they were hungry, that their teeth could tear his flesh more easily than they tore trees, and that alive or dead, he would be eaten by these snails if he permitted it to happen. He drew his hatchet and faced them, conscious that he cut a not very formidable figure with his slight paunch, his pale, skinny legs, his height of five feet seven, about a third the snails' height, but his brows above his glasses were set with a determination to defend his life.

The first snail reared when it was ten feet away. The professor advanced and swung the hatchet at the projecting mantle on the snail's left side. He had not dared get close enough, his aim was inches short, and the weight of the hatchet pulled the professor off balance. He staggered and fell under the raised muzzle, and had just time to roll himself from under the descending mouth before it touched the ground where he had been. Angry now, he circled the snail and swung a blow at the nacreous shell, which turned the blade. The hatchet took an inch-deep chip, but nothing more. The professor swung again, higher this time and in the centre of the shell's posterior, trying for the lung valve beneath, but the valve was still higher, he knew, ten feet from the ground, and once more his hatchet took only a chip. The snail began to turn itself to face him.

The professor then confronted the second snail, rushed at it and swung the hatchet, cutting it in the cheek. The hatchet sank up to its wooden handle, and he had to tug to get it out, and then had to run a few yards, as the snail put on speed and reared its head for a biting attack. Glancing back, the professor saw that no liquid (he had not, of course, expected blood) came from the cut in the snail's cheek, and in fact he couldn't see the cut. And the blow had certainly been no discouragement to the snail's advance.

Professor Clavering began to walk at a sensible pace straight for the snails' lair on the other side of the island. By the time he scrambled down the side of the gulley, he was winded and his legs hurt. But he saw to his relief that the gulley narrowed to a sharp V. Wedged in that, he would be safe. Professor Clavering started into the V, which had an overhanging top rather like a cave, when he saw that what he had taken for some rounded rocks were moving – at least some of them were. They were baby snails! They were larger than good-sized beach balls. And the professor saw, from the way a couple of them were devouring grass blades, that they were hungry.

A snail's head appeared high on his left. The giant parent snail began to descend the gulley. A crepitation, a pair of antennae against the sky on his right, heralded the arrival of the second snail. He had nowhere to turn except the sea, which was not a bad idea, he thought, as these were land snails. The professor waded out and turned left, walking waist-deep in water. It was slow going, and a snail was coming after him. He got closer to the land and ran in thigh-deep water.

The first snail, the darker one, entered the water boldly and crept along in a depth of several inches, showing signs of being willing to go into deeper water when it got abreast of Professor Claveringi. The professor hoped the other snail, maybe the mother, had stayed with the young. But it hadn't. It was following along the land, and accelerating. The professor plunged wildly for the shore where he would be able to move faster.

Now, thank goodness, he saw rocks. Great igneous masses of rocks covered a sloping hill down to the sea. There was bound to be a niche, some place there where he could take shelter. The sun was sinking into the ocean, it would be dark soon, and there was no moon, he knew. The professor was thirsty. When he reached the rocks, he flung himself like a corpse into a trough made by four or five scratchy boulders, which caused him to lie in a curve. The rocks rose two feet above his body, and the trough was hardly a foot wide. A snail couldn't, he reasoned, stick its head down here and bite him.

The peachy curves of the snails' shells appeared, and one, the second, drew closer.

'I'll strike it with my hatchet if it comes!' the professor swore to himself. 'I'll cut its face to ribbons with my knife!' He was now reconciled to killing both adults, because he could take back a pair of the young ones, and in fact more easily because they were smaller.

The snail seemed to sniff like a dog, though inaudibly as its muzzle hovered over the professor's hiding place. Then with majestic calm it came down on the rocks between which the professor lay. Its slimy foot covered the aperture and within seconds had blocked out almost all the light.

Professor Clavering drew his hunting knife in anger and panic, and plunged it several times into the snail's soft flesh. The snail seemed not even to wince. A few seconds later, it stopped moving, though the professor knew that it was not only not dead, as the stabs hadn't touched any vital organs, but that it had fastened itself over his trench in the firmest possible way. No slit of light showed. The professor was only grateful that the irregularity of the rocks must afford a supply of air. Now he pressed frantically with his palms against the snail's body, and felt his hands slip and scrape against rock. The firmness of the snail, his inability to budge it, made him feel slightly sick for a moment.

An hour passed. The professor almost slept, but the experience was more like a prolonged hallucination. He dreamed, or feared, that he was being chewed by twenty thousand pairs of teeth into a heap of mince, which the two giant snails shared with their offspring. To add to his misery, he was cold and hungry. The snail's body gave no warmth, and was even cool.

Some hours later, the professor awoke and saw stars above him. The snail had departed. It was pitch dark. He stood up cautiously, trying not to make a sound, and stepped out of the crevice. He was free! On a sandy stretch of beach a few yards away, Professor Clavering lay down, pressed against a vertical face of rock. Here he slept the remaining hours until dawn.

He awakened just in time, and perhaps not the dawn but a sixth sense had awakened him. The first snail was coming toward him and was only ten feet away. The professor got up on trembling legs, and trotted inland, up a slope. An idea came to him: if he could push a boulder of, say, five hundred pounds

– possible with a lever – on to an adult snail in the gulley, and smash the spot below which its lung lay, then he could kill it. Otherwise, he could think of no other means at his disposal that could inflict a fatal injury. His gun might, but the gun was on the *Samantha*. He had already estimated that it might be a week, or never, that help would come from the Matusas. The *Samantha* would not necessarily float back to the Matusas, would not necessarily be seen by any other ship for days, and even if it was seen, would it be apparent she was drifting? And if so, would the spotters make a beeline for the Matusas to report it? Not necessarily. The professor bent quickly and licked some dew from a leaf. The snails were twenty yards behind him now.

The trouble is, I'm becoming exhausted, he said to himself.

He was even more tired at noon. Only one snail pursued him, but the professor imagined the other resting or eating a tree top, in order to be fresh later. The professor could trot a hundred yards, find a spot to rest in, but he dared not shut his eyes for long, lest he sleep. And he was definitely weak from lack of food.

So the day passed. His idea of dropping a rock down the gulley was thwarted by two factors: the second snail was guarding the gulley now, at the top of its V, and there was no such rock as he needed within a hundred yards.

When dusk came, the professor could not find the hill where the igneous rocks were. Both snails had him in their sight now. His watch said a quarter to seven. Professor Clavering took a deep breath and faced the fact that he must make an attempt to kill one or both snails before dark. Almost without thinking, or planning – he was too spent for that – he chopped down a slender tree and hacked off its branches. The leaves of these branches were devoured by the two snails five minutes after the branches had fallen to the ground. The professor dragged his tree several yards inland, and sharpened one end of it with the hatchet. It was too heavy a weapon for one hand to wield, but in two hands, it made a kind of battering ram, or giant spear.

At once, Professor Clavering turned and attacked, running with the spear pointed slightly upward. He aimed for the first snail's mouth, but struck too low, and the tree end penetrated about four inches into the snail's chest – or the area below its face. No vital organ here, except the long, straight oesophagus, which in these giant snails would be set deeper than four inches. He had nothing for his trouble but lacerated hands. His spear hung for a few seconds in the snail's flesh, then fell out on to the ground. The professor retreated, pulling his hatchet from his belt. The second snail, coming up abreast of the other, paused to chew off a few inches of the tree stump, then joined its mate in giving attention to Professor Clavering. There was something contemptuous, something absolutely assured, about the snails' slow progress toward him, as if they were thinking, 'Escape us a hundred, a thousand times, we shall finally reach you and devour every trace of you.'

The professor advanced once more, circled the snail he had just hit with the tree spear, and swung his hatchet at the rear of its shell. Desperately, he attacked the same spot with five or six direct hits, for now he had a plan. His hacking operation had to be halted, because the second snail was coming up behind him. Its snout and an antenna even brushed the professor's legs moistly and staggered him, before he could step out of its way. Two more hatchet blows the professor got in, and then he stopped, because his right arm hurt. He had by no means gone through the shell, but he had no strength for more effort with the hatchet. He went back for his spear. His target was a small one, but he ran toward it with desperate purpose.

The blow landed. It even broke through.

The professor's hands were further torn, but he was oblivious of them. His success made him as joyous as if he had killed both his enemies, as if a rescue ship with food, water, and a bed were even then sailing into Kuwa's beach.

The snail was twisting and rearing up with pain.

Professor Clavering ran forward, lifted the drooping spear and pushed it with all his might farther into the snail, pointing it upward to go as close as possible to the lung. Whether the snail died soon or not, it was *hors de combat,* the professor saw. And he himself experienced something like physical collapse an instant after seeing the snail's condition. He was quite incapable of taking on the other snail in the same manner, and the other snail was coming after him. The professor tried to walk in a straight line away from both snails, but he weaved with fatigue and faintness. He looked behind him. The unhurt snail was thirty feet away. The wounded snail faced him, but was motionless, half in and half out of its shell, suffering in silence some agony of asphyxiation. Professor Clavering walked on.

Quite by accident, just as it was growing dark, he came upon his field of rocks. Among them he took shelter for the second time. The snail's snout probed the trench in which he lay, but he could not quite reach him. Would it not be better to remain in the trench tomorrow, to hope for rain for water? He fell asleep before he could come to any decision.

Again, when the professor awakened at dawn, the snail had departed. His hands throbbed. Their palms were encrusted with dried blood and sand. He thought it wise to go to the sea and wash them in salt water.

The giant snail lay between him and the sea, and at his approach, the snail very slowly began to creep toward him. Professor Clavering made a wobbling detour and continued on his way toward the water. He dipped his hands and moved them rapidly back and forth, at last lifted water to his face, longed to wet his dry mouth, warned himself that he should not, and yielded anyway, spitting out the water almost at once. Land snails hated salt and could be killed by salt crystals. The professor angrily flung handfuls of water at the snail's face. The snail only lifted its head higher, out of the professor's range. Its form was slender now, and it had, oddly, the grace of a horned gazelle, of some animal of the deer family. The snail lowered its snout, and the professor trudged away, but not quickly enough: the snail came down on his shoulder and the suctorial mouth clamped.

The professor screamed. *My God,* he thought, as a piece of his shirt, a piece of flesh and possibly bone was torn from his left shoulder, *why was I such an ass as to linger?* The snail's weight pushed him under, but it was shallow here, and he struggled to his feet and walked toward the land. Blood streamed hotly down his side. He could not bear to look at his shoulder to see what had happened, and would not have been surprised if his left arm had dropped off in the next instant. The professor walked on aimlessly in shallow water near the land. He was still going faster than the snail.

Then he lifted his eyes to the empty horizon, and saw a dark spot in the water in the mid-distance. He stopped, wondering if it were real or a trick of his eyes: but now he made out the double body of a catamaran, and he thought he saw Dr Stead's straw hat. They had come from the Matusas!

'Hello!' the professor was shocked at the hoarseness, the feebleness of his voice. Not a chance that he had been heard.

But with hope now, the professor's strength increased. He headed for a little beach – not his beach, a smaller one – and when he got there he stood in its centre, his good arm raised, and shouted, 'Dr *Stead*! This way! – On the beach!' He could definitely see Dr Stead's hat and four dark heads.

There was no answering shout. Professor Clavering could not tell if they had heard him or not. And the accursed snail was only thirty feet away now! He'd lost his hatchet, he realized. And the camera that had been under water with him was now ruined, and so were the two pictures in it. No matter. He would live.

'*Here!*' he shouted, again lifting his arm.

The natives heard this. Suddenly all heads in the catamaran turned to him.

Dr Stead pointed to him and gesticulated, and dimly Professor Clavering heard the good doctor urging the boatman to make for the shore. He saw Dr Stead half stand up in the catamaran.

The natives gave a whoop – at first Professor Clavering

83

thought it a whoop of joy, or of recognition, but almost at once a wild swing of the sail, a splash of a couple of oars, told him that the natives were trying to change their course.

Pebbles crackled. The snail was near. And this of course was what the natives had seen – the giant snail.

'*Please – Here!*' the professor screamed. He plunged again into the water. '*Please!*'

Dr Stead was trying, that the professor could see. But the natives were rowing, paddling with hands even, and their sail was carrying them obliquely away.

The snail made a splash as it entered the sea. To drown or to be eaten alive? The professor wondered. He was waist-deep when he stumbled, waist-deep but head under when the snail crashed down upon him, and he realized as the thousands of pairs of teeth began to gnaw at his back, that his fate was both to drown and to be chewed to death.

The Cries of Love

Hattie pulled the little chain of the reading-lamp, drew the covers over her shoulders and lay tense, waiting for Alice's sniffs and coughs to subside. 'Alice?' She said. No response. Yes, she was sleeping already, though she said she never closed an eye before the bedroom clock struck eleven.

Hattie eased herself to the edge of the bed and slowly put out a white-stockinged foot. She twisted round to look at Alice, of whom nothing was visible except a thin nose projecting between the ruffle of her nightcap and the sheet pulled over her mouth. She was still.

Hattie rose gently from the bed, her breath coming short with excitement. In the semi-darkness she could see the two sets of false teeth in their glasses of water on the table. She giggled nervously.

Like a white ghost she made her way across the room, past the Victorian settle. She stopped at the sewing-table, lifted the folding top and groped among the spools and pattern papers until she found the scissors. Then, holding them tightly, she crossed the room again. She had left the wardrobe door slightly ajar earlier in the evening, and it swung open noiselessly. Hattie reached a trembling hand into the blackness, felt the two woollen coats, a few dresses. Finally, she touched a fuzzy thing, and lifted the hanger down. The scissors slipped out of her hand. There was a clatter, followed by half-suppressed laughter.

She peeked round the wardrobe door at Alice, motionless on the bed. Alice was rather hard of hearing.

With her white toes turned up stiffly, Hattie clumped to the easy chair by the window where a bar of moonlight slanted, and sat down with the scissors and the angora cardigan in her lap. In the moonlight her face gleamed, toothless and demoniacal. She examined the cardigan in the manner of a person who toys with a piece of steak before deciding where to put his knife.

It was really a lovely cardigan. Alice had received it the week before from her niece as a birthday present. Alice would never have indulged herself in such a luxury. She was happy as a child with the cardigan and had worn it every day over her dresses.

The scissors cut purringly up the soft wool sleeves, between the wristbands and the shoulders. She considered. There should be one more cut. The back, of course. But only about a foot long, so that it wouldn't immediately be visible.

A few seconds later, she had put the scissors back into the table, hung the cardigan in the wardrobe, and was lying under the covers. She heaved a tremendous sigh. She thought of the gaping sleeves, of Alice's face in the morning. The cardigan was quite beyond repair, and she was immensely pleased with herself.

They were awakened at eight-thirty by the hotel maid. It was a ritual that never failed: three bony raps on the door and a bawling voice with a hint of insolence, 'Eight-thirty. You can get breakfast now!' Then Hattie, who always woke first, would poke Alice's shoulder.

Mechanically they sat up on their respective sides of the bed and pulled their nightgowns over their heads, revealing clean white undergarments. They said nothing. Seven years of co-existence had pared their conversation to an economical core.

This morning, however, Hattie's mind was on the cardigan. She felt self-conscious, but she could think of nothing to say or do to relieve the tension, so she spent more time than usual with her hair. She had a braid nearly two feet long that she wound around her head, and every morning she undid it for its hundred strokes. Her hair was her only vanity. Finally, she stood shifting uneasily, pretending to be fastening the snaps on her dress.

Alice seemed to take an age at the washbasin, gargling with her solution of tepid water and salt. She held stubbornly to water and salt in the mornings, despite Hattie's tempting bottle of red mouthwash sitting on the shelf.

'What are you giggling at now?' Alice turned from the basin, her face wet and smiling a little.

Hattie could say nothing, looked at the teeth in the glass on the bed table and giggled again. 'Here's your teeth.' She reached the glass awkwardly to Alice. 'I thought you were going down to breakfast without them.'

'Now when did I *ever* go off without my teeth, Hattie?'

Alice smiled to herself. It was going to be a good day, she thought. Mrs Crumm and her sister were back from a weekend, and they could all play gin rummy together in the afternoon. She walked to the wardrobe in her stockinged feet.

Hattie watched as she took down the powder-blue dress, the one that went best with the beige angora cardigan. She unfastened all the little buttons in front. Then she took the cardigan from the hanger and put one arm into a sleeve.

'Oh!' she breathed painfully. Then like a hurt child her eyes almost closed and her face twisted petulantly. Tears came quickly down her cheeks. 'H-Hattie.'

Hattie smirked, uncomfortable yet enjoying herself thoroughly. 'Well, I do know!' she exclaimed. 'I wonder who could have done a trick like that!' She went to the bed and sat down, doubled up with laughter.

'Hattie, you did this,' Alice declared in an unsteady voice. She clutched the cardigan to her. 'Hattie, you're just wicked!'

Lying across the bed, Hattie was almost hysterical. 'You know I didn't now, Alice . . . haw-haw! . . . Why do you think I'd – ' Her voice was choked off by uncontrollable laughter. Hattie lay there for several minutes before she was calm enough to go down to breakfast. And when she left the room, Alice was sitting in the big chair by the window, sobbing, her face buried in the angora cardigan.

Alice did not come down until she was called for lunch. She

chatted at the table with Mrs Crumm and her sister and took no notice of Hattie. Hattie sat opposite her, silent and restless, but not at all sorry for what she had done. She could have endured days of indifference on Alice's part without feeling the slightest remorse.

It was a beautiful day. After lunch they went with Mrs Crumm, her sister and the hotel hostess, Mrs Holland, and sat in Gramercy Park.

Alice pretended to be absorbed in her book. It was a detective story by her favourite author, borrowed from the hotel's circulating library. Mrs Crumm and her sister did most of the talking. A weekend trip provided conversation for several afternoons, and Mrs Crumm was able to remember every item of food she had eaten for days running.

The monotonous tones of the voices, the warmth of the sunshine, lulled Alice into half-sleep. The page was blurred to her eyes.

Earlier in the day, she had planned to adopt an attitude toward Hattie. She should be cool and aloof. It was not the first time Hattie had committed an outrage. There had been the ink spilt on her lace tablecloth months ago, the day before she was going to give it to her niece. . . . And her missing volume of Tennyson that was bound in morocco. She was sure Hattie had it, somewhere. She decided that that evening, she should calmly pack her bag, write Hattie a note, short but well-worded, and leave the hotel. She would go to another hotel in the neighbourhood, let it be known through Mrs Crumm where she was, and have the satisfaction of Hattie's coming to her and apologizing. But the fact was, she was not at all sure Hattie would come to her, and this embarrassing possibility prevented her taking such a dangerous course. What if she had to spend the rest of her life alone? It was much easier to stay where she was, to have a pleasant game of gin rummy in the afternoons, and to take out her revenge in little ways. It was also more lady-like, she consoled herself. She did not think beyond this, of the particular times she would say or do things calculated to hurt Hattie. The opportunities would just come of themselves.

Mrs Holland nudged her. 'We're going to get some ice cream now. Then we're going back to play some gin rummy.'

'I was just at the most exciting part of the book.' But Alice rose with the others and was almost cheerful as they walked to the drug store.

Alice won at gin rummy, and felt pleased with herself. Hattie, watching her uneasily all day, was much relieved when she decreed speaking terms again.

Nevertheless, the thought of the ruined cardigan rankled in Alice's mind, and prodded her with a sense of injustice. Indeed, she was ashamed of herself for being able to take it as lightly as she did. It was letting Hattie walk over her. She wished she could muster a really strong hatred.

They were in their room reading at nine o'clock. Every vestige of Hattie's shyness or pretended contrition had vanished. 'Wasn't it a nice day?' Hattie ventured.

'Um-hm.' Alice did not raise her head.

'Well,' Hattie made the inevitable remark through the inevitable yawn, 'I think I'll be going off to bed.'

And a few minutes later they were both in bed, propped up by four pillows. Hattie with the newspaper and Alice with her detective story. They were silent for a while, then Hattie adjusted her pillows and lay down. 'Good night, Alice.'

'Good night.'

Soon Alice pulled out the light, and there was absolute silence in the room except for the soft ticking of the clock and the occasional purr of an automobile. The clock on the mantel whirred and began to strike ten.

Alice lay open-eyed. All day her tears had been restrained, and now she began to cry. But they were not the childish tears of the morning, she felt. She wiped her nose on the top of the sheet.

She raised herself on one elbow. The darkish braid of hair

outlined Hattie's neck and shoulder against the white bed-clothes. She felt very strong, strong enough to murder Hattie with her own hands. But the idea of murder passed from her mind as swiftly as it had entered. Her revenge had to be some-thing that would last, that would hurt, something that Hattie must endure and that she herself could enjoy.

Then it came to her, and she was out of bed, walking boldly to the sewing-table, as Hattie had done twenty-four hours be-fore . . . and she was standing by the bed, bending over Hattie, peering at her placid, sleeping face through her tears and her short-sighted eyes. Two quick strokes of the scissors would cut through the braid, right near the head. But Alice lowered the scissors just a little, to where the braid was tighter. She squeezed the scissors with both hands, made them chew on the braid, as Hattie slowly awakened with the touch of cold metal on her neck. *Whack,* and it was done.

'What is it? . . . What – ?' Hattie said.

The braid was off, lying like a dark grey snake on the bed-cover.

'Alice!' Hattie said, and groped at her neck, felt the stiff ends of the braid's stump. 'Alice!'

Alice stood a few feet away, staring at Hattie who was sitting up in bed, and suddenly Alice was overcome with mirth. She tittered, and at the same time tears started in her eyes. 'You did it to me!' she said. 'You cut my cardigan!'

Alice's instant of self-defence was unnecessary, because Hattie was absolutely crumpled and stunned. She started to get out of bed, as if to go to the mirror, but sat back again, moaning and weeping, feeling of the horried thing at the end of her hair. Then she lay down again, still moaning into her pillow. Alice stayed up, and sat finally in the easy chair. She was full of energy, not sleepy at all. But toward dawn, when Hattie slept, Alice crept between the covers.

Hattie did not speak to her in the morning, and did not look at her. Hattie put the braid away in a drawer. Then she tied a scarf around her head to go down to breakfast, and in the dining-room, Hattie took another table from the one at which Alice and she usually sat. Alice saw Hattie speaking to Mrs Holland after breakfast.

A few minutes later, Mrs Holland came over to Alice, who was reading in a corner of the lounge.

'I think,' Mrs Holland said gently, 'that you and your friend might be happier if you had separate rooms for a while, don't you?'

This took Alice by surprise, though at the same time she had been expecting something worse. Her prepared statement about the spilt ink, the missing Tennyson and the ruined angora subsided in her, and she said quite briskly, 'I do indeed, Mrs Holland. I'm agreeable to anything Hattie wishes.'

Alice offered to move out, but it was Hattie who did. She moved to a smaller room three doors down on the same floor.

That night, Alice could not sleep. It was not that she thought about Hattie particularly, or that she felt in the least sorry for what she had done – she decidedly didn't – but that things, the room, the darkness, even the clock's ticking, were so different because she was alone. A couple of times during the night, she heard a footstep outside the door, and thought it might be Hattie coming back, but it was only people visiting the w.c. at the end of the hall. It occurred to Alice that she could knock on Hattie's door and apologize but, she asked herself, why should she?

In the morning, Alice could tell from Hattie's appearance that she hadn't slept either. Again, they did not speak or look at each other all day, and during the gin rummy and tea at four-thirty, they managed to take different tables. Alice slept very badly that night also, and blamed it on the lamb stew at dinner, which she was having trouble digesting. Hattie would have the same trouble, perhaps, as Hattie's digestion was if anything worse.

Three more days and nights passed, and the ravages of Hattie's and Alice's sleepless nights became apparent on their faces. Mrs Holland noticed and offered Alice some sedatives, which Alice politely declined. She had her pride, she wasn't going to show anyone she was disturbed by Hattie's absence, and besides, she thought it was weak and self-indulgent to yield to sleeping-pills – though perhaps Hattie would.

On the fifth day, at three in the afternoon, Hattie knocked on Alice's door. Her head was still swathed in a scarf, one of three that Hattie possessed, and this was one Alice had given her last Christmas. 'Alice, I want to say I'm sorry, if *you're* sorry,' Hattie said, her lips twisting and pursing as she fought to keep back the tears.

This was or should have been a moment of triumph for Alice. It was, mainly, she felt, though something – she was not sure what – tarnished it a little, made it not quite pure victory. 'I am sorry about your braid, if you're sorry about my cardigan,' Alice replied.

'I am,' said Hattie.

'And about the ink stain on my tablecloth and – where is my volume of Alfred Lord Tennyson's poems?'

'I have not got it,' Hattie said, still tremulous with tears.

'You haven't *got* it?'

'No,' Hattie declared positively.

And in a flash, Alice knew what had really happened: Hattie had at some point, in some place, destroyed it, so it was in a way true now that she hadn't 'got' it. Alice knew, too, that she must not stick over this, that she ought to forgive and forget it, though neither emotionally nor intellectually did she come to this decision: she simply knew and behaved accordingly, saying, 'Very well, Hattie. You may move back, if you wish.'

Hattie then moved back, though at the card game at four-thirty, they still sat at separate tables.

Hattie, having swallowed the biggest lump of pride she had ever swallowed in knocking on Alice's door and saying she was sorry, slept very much better back in the old arrangement, but suffered a lurking sense of unfairness. After all, a book of poems and a cardigan could be replaced, but could her hair? Alice had got back at her all right, and then some. The score was not quite even.

After a few days, Hattie and Alice were back to normal, saying little to each other, but outwardly being congenial, taking meals and playing cards at the same table. Mrs Holland seemed pleased.

It crossed Alice's mind to buy Hattie some expensive hair tonic she saw in a Madison Avenue window one day while on an outing with Mrs Holland and the group. But Alice didn't. Neither did she buy a 'special treatment' for hair which she saw advertised in the back of a magazine, guaranteed to make hair grow thicker and faster, but Alice read every word of the advertisement.

Meanwhile, Hattie struggled in silence with her stump of braid, brushed her hair faithfully as usual, but only when Alice was having her bath or was out of the room, so Alice would not see it. Nothing in Alice's possession now seemed important enough for Hattie's vengeance. But Christmas was coming soon. Hattie determined to wait patiently and see what Alice got then.

Mrs Afton, among Thy Green Braes

For Dr Felix Bauer, staring out the window of his ground-floor office on Lexington Avenue, the afternoon was a sluggish stream that had lost its current, or which might have been flowing either backwards or forwards. Traffic had thickened, but in the molten sunlight cars only inched behind red lights, their chromium twinkling as if with white heat. Dr Bauer's office was air-conditioned, actually pleasantly cool, but something, his logic or his blood, told him it was hot and it depressed him.

He glanced at his wristwatch. Miss Vavrica, who was scheduled for three-thirty, was once more funking her appointment. He could see her now, wide-eyed in a movie theatre probably, hypnotizing herself so as not to think of what she should be doing. There were things he could be doing in the empty minutes before his four-fifteen patient, but he kept staring out the window. What was it about New York, he wondered, for all its speed and ambition, that deprived him of his initiative? He worked hard, he always had, but in America it was with a consciousness of working hard. It was not like Vienna or Paris, where he had worked and lived, relaxed with his wife and friends in the evenings, then found energy for more work, more reading, until the small hours of the morning.

The image of Mrs Afton, small, rather stout but still pretty with a rare, radiant prettiness of middle age – scented, he remembered, with a gardenia cologne – superimposed itself upon the European evenings. Mrs Afton was a very pleasant woman from the American south. She bore out what he had often heard about the American south, that it preserved a tradition of living in which there was time for meals and visits and conversation and, simply, for doing nothing. He had detected it in a few of Mrs Afton's phrases that might not have been necessary but were gratifying to hear, in her quiet good manners – and good manners usually annoyed him – which anxiety had not caused her to forget for an instant. Mrs Afton reflected a way of life which, like an alchemy, made the world into quite another and more beautiful one when he was in her presence. He did not often find such pleasant people among his patients, but then Mrs Afton had come to him last Monday in regard to her husband, not herself.

His four-fifteen patient, earnest Mr Schriever, who earned every penny of the money he paid for his forty-five minute sessions and was aware of it every second, came and went without making a bubble on the afternoon's surface. Alone again, Dr Bauer passed a strong, neat hand over his brows, impatiently smoothed them, and made a final note about Mr Schriever. The young man had talked off the top of his head again, hesitating, then rushing, and no question had been able to steer him into more promising paths. It was such people as Mr Schriever that one had to believe one could finally help. The first barrier was always tension, it seemed to Dr Bauer, not the almost objective tension of war or of poverty that he had found in Europe, but the American kind of tension that was different in each individual and which each seemed to clasp the faster to himself when he came to a psychoanalyst to have it dissected out. Mrs Afton, he recalled, had none of that tension. It was regrettable that a woman born for happiness, reared for it, should be bound to a man who had renounced it. And it was regrettable he could do nothing for her. Today, he had decided, he must tell her he could not help her.

At precisely five, Dr Bauer's foot found the buzzer under the blue carpet, and pressed it twice. He glanced at the door, then got up and opened it.

Mrs Afton came in immediately, her step quick and buoyant for all her plumpness, her carefully waved, light brown head held high. It struck him she was the only creature able to move under its own power that afternoon.

'Good afternoon, Dr Bauer.' She loosened the blue chiffon scarf that did not match but blended with his carpet, and settled herself in the leather armchair. 'It's so divinely cool here! I shall dread leaving today.'

'Yes,' he smiled. 'Air-conditioning spoils one.' Bent over his desk, he read through the notes he had jotted down on Monday:

Thomas Bainbridge Afton, 55. Gen. health good. Irritable. Anxiety about physical strength and training. In recent months, severe diet and exercise programme. Room of hotel suite fitted with gym. equip. Exercises strenuously. Schizoid, sadist-masochist indics. Refuses treatment.

Specifically, Mrs Afton had come to ask him how her husband might be persuaded, if not to stop his regimen, at least to temper it.

Dr Bauer smiled at her uneasily across his desk. He should, he supposed, dismiss her now, explain once more that he could not possibly treat someone through someone else. Mrs Afton had pleaded with him to let her come for a second interview. And she was obviously so much more hopeful now, he found it hard to begin. 'How are things today?' he asked as he always did.

'Very well.' She hesitated. 'I think I've told you almost everything there is to tell. Unless you've something to ask me.' Then, as if realizing her intensity, she leaned back in her chair, blinked her blue eyes and smiled, and the smile seemed to say what she had actually said on Monday, 'I know it's funny, a husband who flexes his arms in front of a mirror like a twelve-year-old boy admiring his muscles, but you can understand that when he trembles from exhaustion afterwards, I fear for his life.'

With the same kind of smile and a nod of understanding, he supposed, if he should begin, 'Since your husband refuses to come personally for treatment . . . ' she would let herself be dismissed, leave his office with her burden of anxiety still within her. Mrs Afton did not spill all her troubles out at once as most middle-aged women of her type did, and she was too proud to admit embarrassing facts as, for instance, that her husband had ever struck her. Dr Bauer felt sure that he had.

'I suspect, of course,' he began, 'that your husband is rebuilding a damaged ego through his physical culture regime. His unconscious reasoning is that having failed in other things – his business, socially perhaps, losing his property in Kentucky, you say, not being as good a provider as he would like to be – he can compensate by being strong physically.'

Mrs Afton looked off and her eyes widened. Dr Bauer had seen them widen before when he challenged her, when she tried to recollect something, and he had seen them narrow suddenly when something amused her, with a flirtatiousness of youth still sparkling through the curved brown lashes. Now the tilt of her head emphasized the wide cheekbones, the narrower forehead, the softly pointed chin – a motherly face, though she had no children. Finally, very dubiously, she replied, 'I suppose that might be logical.'

'But you don't agree?'

'Not entirely, at any rate.' She lifted her head again. 'I don't think my husband considers himself quite a failure. We still live very comfortably, you know.'

'Yes, of course.'

She looked at the electric clock whose second hand swept away silently at the precious forty-five minutes. Her knees parted a little as she leaned forward, and her calves, like an ornamental base, curved symmetrically down to her slender ankles that she kept close together. 'You can't suggest anything that would help me to moderate his – his routine, Dr Bauer?'

'There's not the remotest chance he might be persuaded to see me?'

'I'm afraid not. I told you how he felt about doctors. He says they can tinker with him once he's dead, but he's through with them for the rest of his life. Oh, I don't think I told you that he sold his body to a medical school.' She smiled again, but he saw a twitch of shame or of anger in the smile. 'He did that about six months ago. I thought you might be interested.'

'Yes.'

She went on with the least increase of importunity, 'I do think if you could simply see him for a moment – I mean, if he didn't know who you were, I'm sure you'd be able to learn so much more than I could ever tell you.'

Dr Bauer sighed. 'You see, whatever I could tell you even then would be only guesswork. From you or even from seeing your husband for a few moments, I cannot learn the facts that in the first place caused his obsession with athletics. I might advise you to help him build back what he has lost, his social contacts, his hobbies and so on. But I'm sure you have tried already.'

Mrs Afton conveyed with an uncertain nod that she had tried.

'And still, psychologically, that would be only correcting the surface.'

She said nothing. Her lips tightened at the corners, and she looked off at the four bright yellow echelons the venetian blinds made in a corner of the room. And despite the eagerness of her posture, there was an air of hopelessness now that made Dr Bauer drop his eyes to the capped fountain pen that he rolled under one finger on his desk.

'Still, I'd be so grateful if you'd just try to see him, even if it's only across the lobby of our hotel. Then I'd feel that whatever you said about him was more definite.'

Whatever I say is definite, he thought and abandoned it, his mind going on to what he must say next, that there was nothing for her to do but go to a domestic relations court. The court would probably advise that her husband be taken away for treatment, and Mrs Afton, he knew, would suffer a thousand times more than when he had suggested that her husband had been a failure. She still loved her husband, and divorce was not in her mind, she had said, or even a short separation. Not only still loved him, but was proud of him, Dr Bauer realized. Then suddenly it occurred to him that seeing her husband, glimpsing him, might be the final gesture of courtesy he had been groping for. After he had seen him, he would feel that he had made all the effort possible for him to make.

'I can try it,' he said at last.

'Thank you. I'm sure it will help. I know it will.' She smiled and sat up taller. She shook her head at the cigarette that Dr Bauer extended. 'I'll tell you something else that happened,' she began, and he felt her gratitude radiating toward him. 'I was to see you at two-thirty Monday, you know, so to get away alone, I told Thomas I was to meet Mrs Hatfield – my oldest friend at the hotel – at two-thirty at Lord and Taylor's. Well, I was having lunch in the hotel dining-room by myself at two o'clock, when Thomas came in unexpectedly. We never lunch together, because he goes to a salad bar on Madison Avenue. And there I was having lobster Newburg, which Thomas thinks is the nearest thing to suicide, anyway. Lobster Newburg is a speciality of the hotel on Mondays, and I always order it for lunch. Well, I'd just told Thomas I was to meet Mrs Hatfield at two-thirty, when Mrs Hatfield herself came into the dining-room. She's nearsighted and didn't see us, but my husband saw her as well as I. She sat down at a table and ordered her lunch and obviously she was going to stay there an hour. Thomas just sat opposite me without a word, knowing I'd lied. He's like that sometimes. Then it all comes out at some other time when I'm least expecting it.' She stopped, breathing quickly.

'And it came out – when?' Dr Bauer prompted.

'Yesterday afternoon. He knew positively then that I'd gone to lunch with Mrs Hatfield, because she came upstairs to fetch me. We had lunch with a couple of our friends at the Algonquin. When I came home at about three, Thomas was in a temper and accused me of having gone to see a picture both afternoons, though clearly there hadn't been time to go to a picture after lunch yesterday afternoon.'

'He doesn't like you to go to films?'

She shook her head, laughing, a tolerant laugh that was almost gay. 'The bad air, you know. He thinks all theatres should be torn down. Oh, dear, he is funny sometimes! And he thinks the pictures I like are the lowest form of entertainment. I like a good musical comedy now and then, I must say, and I go when I please.'

Dr Bauer was sure she did not. 'And what else did he say?'

'Well, he didn't say much more, but he threw his gold watch down. It was such a petulant gesture for him, I could hardly believe my eyes.'

She looked at him as if expecting some reaction, then opened her handbag and brought up a gold watch, wrapped its chain once around her forefinger as if to display it to best advantage. As the watch turned, Dr Bauer saw a monogram of interlocked initials on its back.

'It's the watch I gave him the first year we were married. I'm old-fashioned, I suppose, but I like a man to carry a big pocket-watch. By a miracle, it's still running. I'm just taking it now to have a new crystal put in. I simply picked up the watch without saying anything to him, and he put on his coat and went out for his usual afternoon walk. He walks from three till five-thirty or so every day, then comes home and showers – a cold shower – before we go out to dinner together, unless it's one of his evenings with Major Sterns. I told you Major Sterns was Thomas's best friend. They play pinochle or chess together several evenings a week. – Could you possibly see my husband this week, Dr Bauer?'

'I think I can arrange it for Friday noon, Mrs Afton,' he said. He worked at a clinic Friday afternoons, and he could stop by the hotel just before. 'Shall I call you Friday morning? We'll make our plans then. They're always better made quickly.'

She got up when he did, smiling, erect. 'All right. I'll expect your call then. Good day, Dr Bauer. I feel ever so much better. But I'm afraid I've overstayed my time by two minutes.'

He waved his hand protestingly, and held the door open for her. In a moment, she was gone, all but the scent of her cologne that faintly lingered as he stood by his closed door, facing the dusk that had come at the window.

When Dr Bauer arrived at his office the next morning at nine, Mrs Afton had already called twice. She wanted him to call her immediately, his secretary told him, and he meant to as soon as he had hung up his hat, but his telephone buzzed first.

'Can you come this morning?' Mrs Afton asked.

The tremor of fear in her voice alerted him. 'I'm sure I can, Mrs Afton. What has happened?'

'*He* knows I've been seeing you about him. Seeing someone I mean. He accused me of it outright this morning, just after he came back from his morning walk – as if he'd discovered it out of thin air. He accused me of being disloyal to him and packed his suitcases and said he was leaving. He's out now – not with the suitcases, they're still here, so I know he's just walking. He'll probably be back by ten or so. Could you possibly come now?'

'Is he in a violent temper? Has he struck you?'

'Oh, no! Nothing like that. But I know it's the end. I know it can't go on after this.'

Dr Bauer calculated how many appointments he would have to cancel. His ten-fifteen appointment, and possibly his eleven. 'Can you be in the lobby at ten-fifteen?'

'Oh, certainly, Dr Bauer!'

He found it hard to concentrate in his nine-fifteen consultation, and remembering Mrs Afton's voice, he wished he had started off immediately for her hotel. Whatever the circumstances, Mrs Afton had engaged his services, and he was therefore responsible for her.

In a taxi at ten o'clock, he lighted a cigarette and sat motionless, unable to look at the newspaper he had brought with him. Mid-morning of a day in mid-June, he thought, and while he was borne passively in a taxi that continually turned corners and met red lights, Mrs Thomas Bainbridge Afton was at the crisis of more than twenty-five years of marriage. And of what use would he be? To call for help in case of violence, and to utter the usual phrases of comfort, of advice, if her husband had come and gone with his suitcases. It was the end of the gracious, pleasant life of Mrs Afton, who without her husband would never be quite so happy again with her friends. He could hear the remarks she would have made to them: 'Thomas has his peculiarities . . . He has his little fads.' And finally, after embarrassments, compromises, to herself: 'He is impossible.' Yet through pride or breeding or duty, she had maintained, along with her sense of humour, the look of being happily married. 'Thomas is an ideal husband – *was* . . .'

A swerve of the taxi interrupted his thoughts. They had stopped in the middle of a block between Fifth and Sixth Avenues in the Forties, at a hotel smaller and shabbier than he had anticipated, a narrow, tucked-away building that he supposed was filled with middle-aged people like the Aftons, residents of a decade and more.

Mrs Afton walked quickly toward him across the black and white tile floor, and her tense face broke into a smile of welcome. She wiped a handkerchief across her palm and extended her hand. 'How good of you to come, Dr Bauer! He's come back and he's upstairs now. I thought I might introduce you as a friend of a friend of mine – Mr Lanuxe of Charleston. I could say you've just stopped by for a moment before you have to catch a train.'

'As you like.' He followed her toward the elevator, relieved to find her in command of herself.

They entered a tiny, rattling elevator manned by an aged Negro, and were silent as the elevator climbed slowly. Close to her now, Dr Bauer could see traces of grey in her light brown hair, and could hear her overfast breathing. The handkerchief was tightly clenched in one hand.

'It's this way.'

They went along a darkish corridor, down a couple of steps to a different level, and stopped at a tall door.

'I'm sure he's in his own room, but I always knock,' she whispered. Then she opened the door. 'This is the living room.'

Dr Bauer had unconsciously stuffed his newspaper into his jacket pocket so his hands would be free. Now he found himself in an empty, rather depressing room containing hotel furniture, a few books, a brass chandelier that was a spray of former gas pipes, and an undersized black fireplace.

'He's in here,' she said, going toward another door. 'Thomas?' She opened the door cautiously.

There was no answer.

'He isn't in?' Dr Bauer asked.

Mrs Afton seemed embarrassed for a moment. 'He must have stepped out again. But you can come in meanwhile and see what I've been talking to you about. This is his gymnasium, as he calls it.'

Dr Bauer entered a room about half the size of the living-room, and much dimmer, since it had only one fire-escape window. It took him a moment to make out the odd shapes lying on the floor and hanging from the ceiling. There was an ordinary punching bag, a large cylindrical sandbag for tackling or punching, an exercise horse with handgrips, and a couple of basketballs on the floor. He picked up a boxing glove from the floor and the other came with it, fastened by its laces.

'And he has another machine for rowing. It's in the closet there,' Mrs Afton said.

'Can we have more light?'

'Oh, of course.' She pulled a cord and a bare lightbulb came on at the ceiling. 'Any other day, he'd be right here now. I'm sorry. I'm sure he'll be back any minute.'

The laces of the boxing gloves, Dr Bauer saw, were crisp and white, threading only the first eyelets, as if they had never been undone. Under the light now, all the equipment looked brand-new. The exercise horse was dusty, but its leather bore no sign of wear. He frowned at the tan-coloured sandbag only a few inches from his eyes. On the side nearest him, a diamond-shaped paper label was still pasted. Certainly none of the equipment had been used. It was such a surprise to him, he could not at first realize what it meant.

'And there's the mirror.' She pointed to a tall mirror resting on the floor but quite upright against a wall. She chuckled. 'He's eternally in front of that.'

Dr Bauer nodded. Despite her smile, he saw more anxiety in her face than on the afternoon of their first interview, an anxiety that made ugly, tortured ridges of her thin eyebrows. Her hands shook as she picked up a measuring tape and began to roll it neatly around two fingers, awaiting trustfully some comment from him.

'Perhaps I should wait in the lobby,' Dr Bauer murmured.

'All right. I'll call down and have you paged when he comes in. He always uses the stairs. I suppose that's how we missed him when he went out.'

The stairway was directly in front of Dr Bauer when he went out into the hall, so he took it, dazedly. A slight blond man came up the stairs, seemed to eye him a moment before he passed him, but Dr Bauer was sure it could not be he. He felt stunned, without knowing exactly what had stunned him. In the lobby, he looked one way then the other, and finally went to the desk that was half hidden under a different set of stairs.

'You have a Mrs Afton registered here,' he said, stating it more than asking.

The young man at the switchboard looked up from his newspaper. 'Afton? No, sir.'

'Mrs Afton in room thirty-two.'

'No, sir. No Afton here at all.'

'Then who is it in room thirty-two?' At least he was sure of the room number.

The young man checked quickly with his list over the switchboard. 'That's Miss Gorham's suite.' And slowly, as he looked at Dr Bauer, his empty face took on a smile of amusement.

'Miss Gorham? She's not married?' Dr Bauer moistened his lips. 'She lives by herself?'

'Yes, sir.'

'Do you know the person I mean? A woman about fifty, somewhat plump, light brown hair?' he knew, he knew, but he had to make doubly sure.

'Miss Gorham, yes. Miss Frances Gorham.'

Dr Bauer looked into the smiling eyes of the young man

who knew Miss Gorham, and wondered what the clerk knew that he didn't. Many a time Mrs Afton must have smiled at this young man, too, ingratiated herself as she had with him in his office. 'Thank you,' he said. Then absently, 'Nothing more.'

He faced in the other direction, staring at nothing, setting his teeth until the sensation of reality's crumbling stopped and the world righted itself again and became hard, a little shabby like the hotel lobby, as definite as the sound of grit under a passerby's heel on the tile floor, until there was no more Mrs Afton. He was walking toward the door, when a compulsion to return to routine made him look at his wristwatch, made him realise he could be back for his eleven o'clock appointment after all, because it was scarcely ten-forty. He veered toward the coffin-like form of a telephone booth that was nearly hidden behind a large jar of palms. A shelf with telephone directories was at the side under a light, and some stubborn, senseless curiosity prompted him to turn to the A's in the Manhattan directory, to look for Afton. There was only one Afton, and that was the trade name of some kind of shop. He entered the booth and dialled his office number.

'Would you try to reach Mr Schriever again,' he told his secretary, 'and ask him if he can still come at eleven. With my apologies for the changes. And when is Mrs Afton's next appointment?'

'Just a moment. We have her tentatively scheduled for two-thirty Monday.'

'Would you change that, please, to an appointment for Miss Gorham?' he said distinctly. 'Miss Frances Gorham for the same time?'

'Gorham? 'That's G-o-r-h-a-m?'

'Yes. I suppose so.'

'That's a new patient, Dr Bauer?'

'Yes,' he said.

The Heroine

The girl was so sure she would get the job, she had unabashedly come out to Westchester with her suitcase. She sat in a comfortable chair in the living-room of the Christiansens' house, looking in her navy-blue coat and beret even younger than twenty-one, and replied earnestly to their questions.

'Have you worked as a governess before?' Mr Christiansen asked. He sat beside his wife on the sofa, his elbows on the knees of his grey flannel trousers, and his hands clasped. 'Any references, I mean?'

'I was a maid in Mrs Dwight Howell's house in New York for the last seven months.' Lucille looked at him with suddenly wide grey eyes. 'I could get a reference from there if you like . . . But when I saw your advertisement this morning, I didn't want to wait. I've always wanted a place where there were children.'

Mrs Christiansen smiled, but mainly to herself, at the girl's enthusiasm. She took a silver box from the coffee table, stood up and offered it to the girl. 'Will you have one?'

'No, thank you. I don't smoke.'

'Well,' Mrs Christiansen said, lighting her own cigarette, 'we might call them, of course, but my husband and I set more store by appearances than references . . . What do you say, Ronald? You told me you wanted someone who really liked children.'

And fifteen minutes later, Lucille Smith was standing in her room in the servants' quarters back of the house, buttoning the belt of her new white uniform. She touched her mouth lightly with lipstick. 'You're starting all over again, Lucille,' she told herself in the mirror. 'You're going to have a happy, useful life from now on, and forget everything that was before.'

But there went her eyes too wide again, as if to deny her words. Her eyes looked much like her mother's when they opened like that, and her mother was part of what she must forget. She must overcome that habit of stretching her eyes. It made her look surprised and uncertain, too, which was not at all the way to look around children. Her hand trembled as she set the lipstick down. She recomposed her face in the mirror, smoothed the starched front of her uniform. There were only a few things like the eyes to remember, a few silly habits, really, like burning little bits of paper in ash trays, forgetting time sometimes – little things that many people did, but that she must remember not to do. With practice the remembering would come automatically. Because she was just like other people (had the psychiatrist not told her so?), and other people never thought of them at all.

She crossed the room, sank on to the windowseat under the blue curtains, and looked out on the garden and lawn that lay between the servants' house and the big house. The yard was longer than it was wide, with a round fountain in the centre and two flagstone walks lying like a crooked cross in the grass. There were benches here and there, against a tree, under an arbour, that seemed to be made of white lace. A beautiful yard!

And the house was the house of her dreams! A white, two-storey house with dark-red shutters, with oaken doors and brass knockers and latches that opened with a press of the thumb . . . and broad lawns and poplar trees so dense and high one could not see through, so that one did not have to admit or believe that there was another house somewhere beyond . . . The rain-streaked Howell house in New York, granite pillared and heavily ornamented, had looked, Lucille thought, like a stale wedding cake in a row of other stale wedding cakes . . .

She rose suddenly from her seat. The Christiansen house was blooming, friendly, and alive! There were children in it. Thank God for the children! But she had not even met them yet.

She hurried downstairs, crossed the yard on the path that ran from the door, lingered a few seconds to watch the plump faun blowing water from his reeds into the rock pond . . . What was it the Christiansens had agreed to pay her? She did not remember and she did not care. She would have worked for nothing just to live in such a place.

Mrs Christiansen took her upstairs to the nursery. She opened the door of a room whose walls were decorated with bright peasant designs, dancing couples and dancing animals, and twisting trees in blossom. There were twin beds of buff-coloured oak, and the floor was yellow linoleum, spotlessly clean.

The two children lay on the floor in one corner, amid scattered crayons and picture books.

'Children, this is your new nurse,' their mother said. 'Her name is Lucille.'

The little boy stood up and said, 'How do you do,' as he solemnly held out a crayon-stained hand.

Lucille took it, and with a slow nod of her head repeated his greeting.

'And Heloise,' Mrs Christiansen said, leading the second child, who was smaller, toward Lucille.

Heloise stared up at the figure in white and said, 'How do you do.'

'Nicky is nine and Heloise six,' Mrs Christiansen told her.

'Yes,' Lucille said. She noticed that both children had a touch of red in their blond hair, like their father. Both wore blue overalls without shirts, and their backs and shoulders were sun-brown beneath the straps. Lucille could not take her eyes from them. They were the perfect children of her perfect house. They looked up at her frankly, with no mistrust, no hostility. Only love, and some childlike curiosity.

' . . . and most people do prefer living where there's more country,' Mrs Christiansen was saying.

'Oh, yes . . . yes, ma'am. It's ever so much nicer here than in the city.'

Mrs Christiansen was smoothing the little girl's hair with

a tenderness that fascinated Lucille. 'It's just about time for their lunch,' she said. 'You'll have your meals up here, Lucille. And would you like tea or coffee or milk?'

'I'd like coffee, please.'

'All right, Lisabeth will be up with the lunch in a few minutes.' She paused at the door. 'You aren't nervous about anything, are you, Lucille?' she asked in a low voice.

'Oh, no ma'am.'

'Well, you mustn't be.' She seemed about to say something else, but she only smiled and went out.

Lucille stared after her, wondering what that something else might have been.

'You're a lot prettier than Catherine,' Nicky told her.

She turned around. 'Who's Catherine?' Lucille seated herself on a hassock, and as she gave all her attention to the two children who still gazed at her, she felt her shoulders relax their tension.

'Catherine was our nurse before. She went back to Scotland ... I'm glad you're here. We didn't like Catherine.'

Heloise stood with her hands behind her back, swaying from side to side as she regarded Lucille. 'No,' she said, 'We didn't like Catherine.'

Nicky stared at his sister. 'You shouldn't say that. That's what I said!'

Lucille laughed and hugged her knees. Then Nicky and Heloise laughed, too.

A coloured maid entered with a steaming tray and set it on the blond wood table in the centre of the room. She was slender and of indefinite age. 'I'm Lisabeth Jenkins, miss,' she said shyly as she laid some paper napkins at three places.

'My name's Lucille Smith,' the girl said.

'Well, I'll just leave you to do the rest, miss. If you need anything else, just holler.' she went out, her hips small and hard-looking under the blue uniform.

The three sat down to the table, and Lucille lifted the cover from the large dish, exposing three parsley-garnished omelettes, bright yellow in the bar of sunlight that crossed the table.

But first there was tomato soup for her to ladle out, and triangles of buttered toast to pass. Her coffee was in a silver pot, and the children had two large glasses of milk. The table was low for Lucille, but she did not mind. It was so wonderful merely to be sitting here with these children, with the sun warm and cheerful on the yellow linoleum floor, on the table, on Heloise's ruddy face opposite her. How pleasant not to be in the Howell house! She had always been clumsy there. But here it would not matter if she dropped a pewter cover or let a gravy spoon fall in someone's lap. The children would only laugh.

Lucille sipped her coffee.

'Aren't you going to eat?' Heloise asked, with her mouth already full.

The cup slipped in Lucille's fingers, and she spilled half her coffee on the cloth. No, it was not cloth, thank goodness, but oilcloth. She could get it up with a paper towel, and Lisa-beth would never know.

'Piggy!' laughed Heloise.

'Heloise!' Nicky admonished, and went to fetch some paper towels from the bathroom.

They mopped up together.

'Dad always gives us a little of his coffee,' Nicky remarked as he took his place again.

Lucille had been wondering whether the children would mention the accident to their mother. She sensed that Nicky was offering her a bribe. 'Does he?' she asked.

'He pours a little in our milk,' Nicky went on, 'just so you can see the colour.'

'Like this?' And Lucille poured a bit from the graceful silver spout into each glass.

The children gasped with pleasure. 'Yes!'

'Mother doesn't like us to have coffee,' Nicky explained, 'But when she's not looking, Dad let's us have a little like you did. Dad says his day wouldn't be any good without his coffee, and I'm the same way . . . Gosh, Catherine wouldn't give us any coffee like that, would she, Heloise?'

'Not her!' Heloise took a long, delicious draught from her glass which she held with both hands.

Lucille felt a glow rise from deep inside her until it settled in her face and burned there. The children liked her, there was no doubt of that. She remembered how often she had gone to the public parks in the city, during the three years she had worked as maid in various houses (to be a maid was all she was fit for, she used to think), merely to sit on a bench and watch the children play. But the children there had usually been dirty or foul-mouthed, and she herself had always been an outsider. Once she had seen a mother slap her own child across the face. She remembered how she had fled in pain and horror . . .

'Why do you have such big eyes?' Heloise demanded.

Lucille started. 'My mother had big eyes, too,' she said deliberately, like a confession.

'Oh,' Heloise replied, satisfied.

Lucille cut slowly into the omelette she did not want. Her mother had been dead three weeks now. Only three weeks and it seemed much, much longer. That was because she was forgetting, she thought, forgetting all the hopeless hope of the last three years, that her mother might recover in the sanatorium. But recover to what? The illness was something separate, something which had killed her. It had been senseless to hope for a complete sanity which she knew her mother had never had. Even the doctors had told her that. And they had told her other things, too, about herself. Good, encouraging things they were, that she was as normal as her father had been. Looking at Heloise's friendly little face across from her, Lucille felt the comforting glow return. Yes, in this perfect house, closed from all the world, she could forget and start anew.

'Are we ready for some Jello?' she asked.

Nicky pointed to her plate. 'You're not finished eating.'

'I wasn't very hungry.' Lucille divided the extra dessert between them.

'We could go out to the sandbox now,' Nicky suggested. 'We always go just in the mornings, but I want you to see our castle.'

The sandbox was in the back of the house in a corner made by a projecting ell. Lucille seated herself on the wooden rim of the box while the children began piling and patting like gnomes.

'I must be the captured princess!' Heloise shouted.

'Yes, and I'll rescue her, Lucille. You'll see!'

The castle of moist sand rose rapidly. There were turrets with tin flags sticking from their tops, a moat, and a draw-bridge made of the lid of a cigar box covered with sand. Lucille watched, fascinated. She remembered vividly the story of Brian de Bois-Guilbert and Rebecca. She had read *Ivanhoe* through at one long sitting, oblivious of time and place just as she was now.

When the castle was done, Nicky put half a dozen marbles inside it just behind the drawbridge. 'These are good soldiers imprisoned,' he told her. He held another cigar box lid in front of them until he had packed up a barrier of sand. Then he lifted the lid and the sand door stood like a porte-cochère.

Meanwhile Heloise gathered ammunition of small pebbles from the ground next to the house. 'We break the door down and the good soldiers come down the hill across the bridge. Then I'm saved!'

'Don't tell her! She'll see!'

Seriously Nicky thumped the pebbles from the rim of the sandbox opposite the castle door, while Heloise behind the castle thrust a hand forth to repair the destruction as much as she could between shots, for besides being the captured princess she was the defending army.

Suddenly Nicky stopped and looked at Lucille. 'Dad knows how to shoot with a stick. He puts the rock on one end and hits the other. That's a balliska.'

'Ballista,' Lucille said.

'Golly, how did *you* know?'

'I read about it in a book – about castles.'

'Golly!' Nicky went back to his thumping, embarrassed that

he had pronounced the word wrong. 'We got to get the good soldiers out fast. They're captured, see? Then when they're released that means we can all fight together and *take the castle*!

'And save the princess!' Heloise put in.

As she watched, Lucille found herself wishing for some real catastrophe, something dangerous and terrible to befall Heloise, so that she might throw herself between her and the attacker, and prove her great courage and devotion . . . She would be seriously wounded herself, perhaps with a bullet or a knife, but she would beat off the assailant. Then the Christiansens would love her and keep her with them always. If some madman were to come upon them suddenly now, someone with a loose mouth and bloodshot eyes, she would not be afraid for an instant.

She watched the sand wall crumble and the first good soldier marble struggled free and came wobbling down the hill. Nicky and Heloise whooped with joy. The wall gave way completely, and two, three, four soldiers followed the first, their stripes turning gaily over the sand. Lucille leaned forward. Now she understood! She was like the good soldiers imprisoned in the castle. The castle was the Howell house in the city, and Nicky and Heloise had set her free. She was free to do good deeds. And now if only something would happen . . .

'O-o-ow!'

It was Heloise. Nicky had mashed one of her fingers against the edge of the box as they struggled to get the same marble.

Lucille seized the child's hand, her heart thumping at the sight of the blood that rose from many little points in the scraped flesh. 'Heloise, does it hurt very much?'

'Oh, she wasn't supposed to touch the marbles in the first place!' Disgruntled, Nicky sat in the sand.

Lucille held her handkerchief over the finger and half carried her into the house, frantic lest Lisabeth or Mrs Christiansen see them. She took Heloise into the bathroom that adjoined the nursery, and in the medicine cabinet found mercurochrome and gauze. Gently she washed the finger. It was only a small scrape, and Heloise stopped her tears when she saw how slight it was.

'See, it's just a little scratch!' Lucille said, but that was only to calm the child. To her it was not a little scratch. It was a terrible thing to happen the first afternoon she was in charge, a catastrophe she had failed to prevent. She wished over and over that the hurt might be on her own hand, twice as severe.

Heloise smiled as she let the bandage be tied. 'Don't punish Nicky,' she said. 'He didn't mean to do it. He just plays rough.'

But Lucille had no idea of punishing Nicky. She wanted only to punish herself, to seize a stick and thrust it into her own palm.

'Why do you make your teeth like that?'

'I – I thought it might be hurting you.'

'It doesn't hurt any more.' And Heloise went skipping out of the bathroom. She leaped on to her bed and lay on the tan cover that fitted the corners and came all the way to the floor. Her bandaged finger showed startlingly white against the brown of her arm. 'We have to take a nap now,' she told Lucille, and closed her eyes. 'Good-bye.'

'Good-bye,' Lucille answered, and tried to smile.

She went down to get Nicky and when they came up the stairs Mrs Christiansen was at the nursery door.

Lucille blanched. 'I don't think it's bad, ma'am. It – It's a scratch from the sandbox.'

'Heloise's finger? Oh, no, don't worry, my dear. They're always getting little scratches. It does them good. Makes them more careful.'

Mrs Christiansen went in and sat on the edge of Nicky's bed. 'Nicky, dear, you must learn to be more gentle. Just see how you frightened Lucille!' She laughed and ruffled his hair.

Lucille watched from the doorway. Again she felt herself an outsider, but this time because of her incompetence. Yet how different this was from the scenes she had watched in the parks!

Mrs Christiansen patted Lucille's shoulder as she went out. 'They'll forget all about it by nightfall.'

'Nightfall,' Lucille whispered as she went back into the nursery. 'What a beautiful word!'

While the children slept, Lucille looked through an illustrated book of *Pinocchio*. She was avid for stories, any kind of stories, but most of all adventure stories and fairy tales. And at her elbow on the children's shelf there were scores of them. It would take her months to read them all. It did not matter that they were for children. In fact, she found that kind more to her liking, because such stories were illustrated with pictures of animals dressed up, and tables and houses and all sorts of things come to life.

Now she turned the pages of *Pinocchio* with a sense of contentment and happiness so strong that it intruded upon the story she was reading. The doctor at the sanatorium had encouraged her reading, she remembered, and had told her to go to movies, too. 'Be with normal people and forget all about your mother's difficulties . . . ' (Difficulties, he had called it then, but all other times he had said strain. Strain it was, like a thread, running through the generations. She had thought, through her.) Lucille could still see the psychiatrist's face, his head turned a little to one side, his glasses in his hand as he spoke, just as she had thought a psychiatrist should look. 'Just because your mother had a strain, there's no reason why you should not be as normal as your father was. I have every reason to believe you are. You are an intelligent girl, Lucille . . . Get yourself a job out of the city . . . relax . . . enjoy life . . . I want you to forget even the house your family lived in . . . After a year in the country . . . '

That, too, was three weeks ago, just after her mother had died in the ward. And what the doctor had said was true. In this house where there were peace and love, beauty and children, she could feel the moils of the city sloughing off her like a snake's outworn skin. Already, in this one half day! In a week she would forget for ever her mother's face.

With a little gasp of joy that was almost ecstasy she turned
to the bookshelf and chose at random six or seven tall, slender,
brightly coloured books. One she laid open, face down, in her
lap. Another she opened and leaned against her breast. Still
holding the rest in one hand, she pressed her face into *Pinocchio's* pages, her eyes half closed. Slowly she rocked back and
forth in the chair, conscious of nothing but her own happiness
and gratitude. The chimes downstairs struck three times, but
she did not hear them.

'What are you doing?' Nicky asked, his voice politely curious.

Lucille brought the book down from her face. When the
meaning of his question struck her, she flushed and smiled like
a happy but guilty child. 'Reading!' she laughed.

Nicky laughed, too. 'You read awful close.'

'Ya-yuss,' said Heloise, who had also sat up.

Nicky came over and examined the books in her lap. 'We
get up at three o'clock. Would you read to us now? Catherine
always read to us until dinner.'

'Shall I read to you out of *Pinocchio*?' Lucille suggested,
happy that she might possibly share with them the happiness
she had gained from the first pages of its story. She sat down
on the floor so they could see the pictures as she read.

Nicky and Heloise pushed their eager faces over the pictures,
and sometimes Lucille could hardly see to read. She did not
realize that she read with a tense interest that communicated
itself to the two children, and that this was why they enjoyed it
so much. For two hours she read, and the time slipped by almost
like so many minutes.

Just after five Lisabeth brought in the tray with their dinner,
and when the meal was over Nicky and Heloise demanded
more reading until their bedtime at seven. Lucille gladly began
another book, but when Lisabeth returned to remove the tray,
she told Lucille that it was time for the children's bath, and
that Mrs Christiansen would be up to say good night in a little
while.

Mrs Christiansen was up at seven, but the two children by

that time were in their robes, freshly bathed, and deep in another story with Lucille on the floor.

'You know,' Nicky said to his mother, 'we've read all these books before with Catherine, but when Lucille reads them they seem like *new* books!'

Lucille flushed with pleasure. When the children were in bed, she went downstairs with Mrs Christiansen.

'Is everything fine, Lucille? . . . I thought there might be something you'd like to ask me about the running of things.'

'No, ma'am, except . . . might I come up once in the night to see how the children are doing?'

'Oh, I wouldn't want you to break your sleep, Lucille. That's very thoughtful, but it's really unnecessary.'

Lucille was silent.

'And I'm afraid the evenings are going to seem long to you. If you'd ever like to go to a picture in town, Alfred, that's the chauffeur, he'll be glad to take you in the car.'

'Thank you, ma'am.'

'Then good night, Lucille.'

'Good night, ma'am.'

She went out the back way, across the garden where the fountain was still playing. And when she put her hand on the knob of her door, she wished that it were the nursery door, that it were eight o'clock in the morning and time to begin another day.

Still she was tired, pleasantly tired. How very pleasant it was, she thought, as she turned out the light, to feel properly tired in the evening (although it was only nine o'clock) instead of bursting with energy, instead of being unable to sleep for thinking of her mother or worrying about herself . . . She remembered one day not so long ago when for fifteen minutes she had been unable to think of her name. She had run in panic to the doctor . . .

That was past! She might even ask Alfred to buy her a pack of cigarettes in town – a luxury she had denied herself for months.

She took a last look at the house from her window. The

curtains in the nursery billowed out now and then and were swept back again. The wind spoke in the nodding tops of the poplars like friendly voices, like the high-pitched, ever rippling voices of children . . .

The second day was like the first, except that there was no mishap, no scraped hand – and the third and the fourth. Regular and identical like the row of Nicky's lead soldiers on the playtable in the nursery. The only thing that changed was Lucille's love for the family and the children – a blind and passionate devotion which seemed to redouble each morning. She noticed and loved many things: the way Heloise drank her milk in little gulps at the back of her throat, how the blond down on their backs swirled up to meet the hair on the napes of their necks, and when she bathed them the painful vulnerability of their bodies.

Saturday evening she found an envelope addressed to herself in the mailbox at the door of the servants' house. Inside was a blank sheet of paper and inside that a couple of new twenty-dollar bills. Lucille held one of them by its crisp edges. Its value meant nothing to her. To use it she would have to go to stores where other people were. What use had she for money if she were never to leave the Christiansen home? It would simply pile up, forty dollars each week. In a year's time she would have two thousand and eighty dollars, and in two years' time twice that. Eventually she might have as much as the Christiansens themselves and that would not be right.

Would they think it very strange if she asked to work for nothing? Or for ten dollars perhaps?

She had to speak to Mrs Christiansen, and she went to her the next morning. It was an inopportune time. Mrs Christiansen was making up a menu for a dinner.

'Yes?' Mrs Christiansen said in her pleasant voice.

Lucille watched the yellow pencil in her hand moving swiftly over the paper. 'It's too much for me, ma'am.'

The pencil stopped. Mrs Christiansen's lips parted slightly in surprise. 'You *are* such a funny girl, Lucille!'

'How do you mean – funny?' Lucille asked curiously.

'Well, first you want to be practically day and night with the children. You never even want your afternoon off. You're always talking about doing something "important" for us, though what that could be I can't imagine . . . And now your salary's too much! We've never had a girl like you, Lucille. I can assure you, you're different!' She laughed, and the laugh was full of ease and relaxation that contrasted with the tension of the girl who stood before her.

Lucille was rapt by the conversation. 'How do you mean different, ma'am?'

'Why, I've just told you, my dear. And I refuse to lower your salary because that would be sheer exploitation. In fact, if you ever change your mind and want a raise –'

'Oh, no, ma'am . . . but I just wish there was something more I could do for you . . . all of you . . .'

'Lucille! You're working for us, aren't you? Taking care of our children. What could be more important than that?'

'But I mean something bigger – I mean more –'

'Nonsense, Lucille,' Mrs Christiansen interrupted. 'Just because the people you were with before were not so – friendly as we are doesn't mean you have to work your fingers to the bone for us.' She waited for the girl to make some move to go, but she still stood by the desk, her face puzzled. 'Mr Christiansen and I are very well pleased with you, Lucille.'

'Thank you, ma'am.'

She went back to the nursery where the children were playing. She had not made Mrs Christiansen understand. If she could just go back and explain what she felt, tell her about her mother and her fear of herself for so many months, how she had never dared take a drink or even a cigarette . . . and how just being with the family in this beautiful house had made her well again . . . telling her all that might relieve her. She turned toward the door, but the thought of disturbing her or boring her with the story, a servant girl's story, made her stop. So during the rest of the day she carried her unexpressed gratitude like a great weight in her breast.

That night she sat in her room with the light on until

after twelve o'clock. She had her cigarettes now, and she allowed herself three in the evening, but even those were sufficient to set her blood tingling, to relax her mind, to make her dream heroic dreams. And when the three cigarettes were smoked, and she would have liked another, she rose very light in the head and put the cigarette pack in her top drawer to close away temptation. Just as she slid the drawer she noticed on her handkerchief box the two twenty-dollar bills the Christiansens had given her. She took them now, and sat down again in her chair.

From the book of matches she took a match, struck it, and leaned it, burning end down, against the side of her ashtray. Slowly she struck matches one after another and laid them strategically to make a tiny, flickering, well-controlled fire. When the matches were gone, she tore the pasteboard cover into little bits and dropped them in slowly. Finally she took the twenty-dollar bills and with some effort tore bits from them of the same size. These, too, she meted to the fire.

Mrs Christiansen did not understand, but if she saw *this,* she might. Still *this* was not enough. Mere faithful service was not enough either. Anyone would give that, for money. She was different. Had not Mrs Christiansen herself told her that? Then she remembered what else she had said: 'Mr Christiansen and I are very well pleased with you, Lucille.'

The memory of those words brought her up from her chair with an enchanted smile upon her lips. She felt wonderfully strong and secure in her own strength of mind and her position in the household. *Mr Christiansen and I are very well pleased with you, Lucille.* There was really only one thing lacking in her happiness. She had to prove herself in crisis.

If only a plague like those she had read of in the Bible . . . 'And it came to pass that there was a great plague over all the land.' That was how the Bible would say it. She imagined waters lapping higher against the big house, until they swept almost into the nursery. She would rescue the children and swim with them to safety, wherever that might be.

She moved restlessly about the room.

Or if there came an earthquake . . . She would rush in among falling walls and drag the children out. Perhaps she would go back for some trifle, like Nicky's lead soldiers or Heloise's paint set, and be crushed to death. Then the Christiansens would know her devotion.

Or if there might be a fire. Anyone might have a fire. Fires were common things and needed no wrathful visitations from the upper world. There might be a terrible fire just with the gasoline in the garage and a match.

She went downstairs, through the inside door that opened to the garage. The tank was three feet high and entirely full, so that unless she had been inspired with the necessity and importance of her deed, she would not have been able to lift the thing over the threshold of the garage and of the servants' house, too. She rolled the tank across the yard in the same manner as she had seen men roll beer barrels and ashcans. It made no noise on the grass and only a brief bump and rumble over one of the flagstone paths, lost in the night.

No lights shone at any of the windows, but if they had, Lucille would not have been deterred. She would not have been deterred had Mr Christiansen himself been standing there by the fountain, for probably she would not have seen him. And if she had, was she not about to do a noble thing? No, she would have seen only the house and the children's faces in the room upstairs.

She unscrewed the cap and poured some gasoline on a corner of the house, rolled the tank farther, poured more against the white shingles, and so on until she reached the far corner. Then she struck her match and walked back the way she had come, touching off the wet places. Without a backward glance she went to stand at the door of the servants' house and watch.

The flames were first pale and eager, then they became yellow with touches of red. As Lucille watched, all the tension that was left in her, in body or mind, flowed evenly upward and was lifted from her for ever, leaving her muscles and brain free for the voluntary tension of an athlete before a starting gun. She would let the flames leap tall, even to the nursery window, before she rushed in, so that the danger might be at its highest. A smile like that of a saint settled on her mouth, and anyone seeing her there in the doorway, her face glowing in the lambent light, would certainly have thought her a beautiful young woman.

She had lit the fire at five places, and these now crept up the house like the fingers of a hand, warm and flickering, gentle and caressing. Lucille smiled and held herself in check. Then suddenly the gasoline tank, having grown too warm, exploded with a sound like a cannon and lighted the entire scene for an instant.

As though this had been the signal for which she waited, Lucille went confidently forward.

Another Bridge to Cross

The top of the car was down, and Merrick saw the man on the bridge from a good mile away. The car in which Merrick rode was speeding toward him, and Merrick thought: 'It's like something in a Bergman film. The man has a gun in his hand now, and when the car gets so near the bridge he can't miss, he'll fire at me, I'll be hit through the chest, and that's probably just as well.' Merrick kept looking at the hunched figure on the bridge – the man was leaning on his forearms on the rail – both because he expected catastrophe, and because the man on the bridge was the only human figure in the landscape to look at. They were in Italy on the southern Riviera. The Mediterranean's serene blueness lay on their left, and on the right powdery green olive fields, that looked in need of water, straggled up the hills until stopped by the rocky feet of mountains. The bridge spanned the road, carried a crossroad, and was at least three storeys high.

But the man did not move as Merrick's car reached the bridge. Merrick saw a breeze stir his dark hair. The danger was over.

Then above the roar of an oncoming truck, Merrick heard a faint thud, as if a sandbag had fallen off the back of the car. He turned around, raising himself slightly. 'Stop!' he shouted to his driver.

A dark blob lay on the road under the bridge, and Merrick looked around just in time to see the truck pass over it with the left pairs of its enormous double tyres. The truck then screeched to a halt. The driver was getting out. Merrick pulled his hand down his forehead, over his eyes.

'What happened?' asked Merrick's driver, yanking his sunglasses off, squinting behind him to see. He backed the car.

'A man was killed,' Merrick said.

The driver backed the car neatly to the extreme right-hand side of the road, pulled the handbrake, and jumped out.

For a few moments, the driver and the truck driver had an animated conversation which Merrick could not hear. Merrick did not get out of the car. The truck driver had pulled the body on to the grass at the side of the road. No doubt he was explaining to Merrick's driver that he could not possibly have stopped, because the man jumped right in front of him.

'*Dio mio*,' Merrick's driver said, coming back, getting into the car. 'A suicide. Not an old man, either.' The driver shook his head.

Merrick said nothing.

They drove on.

After ten minutes, the driver said, 'A pity you don't like Amalfi, sir.'

'Yes. Well – ' Merrick was in no mood for talking. His Italian was limited to a basic vocabulary, which however he knew thoroughly and pronounced correctly. Amalfi was where he had had his honeymoon twenty-five years ago. No use mentioning that to an Italian from Messina who was only about thirty himself.

They stopped at a village Merrick had seen on the map in Palmero and inquired about. The tourist agent had said, 'Very pretty, very quiet,' so Merrick intended to try it. He had telephoned from Messina and booked a room and bath. The driver took him to the hotel, and Merrick paid him off, tipping him so well the driver broke into a big smile.

'Many thanks, sir. May you enjoy your holiday here!' Then he was gone, back to Messina.

The Hotel Paradiso was very pretty, but not what Merrick wanted. He knew this after two minutes' inspection of its main hall with its inner court of little fruit trees and a sixteenth-century well, open to the sky. The tiles of the floors were lovely, the view from his window of the Mediterranean as commanding as that from the bridge of a ship, but it was not what he wanted. Nevertheless, Merrick stayed the night, and the next morning hired a car to go on. While he waited in the hotel for the car to arrive, he looked in the small local newspaper for anything about the man who had jumped from the bridge.

It was a short one-column item on the second page. His name was Dino Bartucci, 32, unemployed mason, with a wife and five children (their names and ages were given, all were under ten); his wife was in poor health, and Bartucci had been extremely depressed and anxious for many months. He had twice said to friends, 'If I were dead, the State would at least give my wife and children a small pension.'

Merrick knew how small that pension must be. There was the extreme, Merrick thought, of human anxiety: poverty, a sick wife, hungry children, and no work. And he found it mysterious that he had correctly anticipated death as soon as he saw the man, but that he had imagined it turned against himself.

Merrick got into the car with the new driver. At one, they reached Amalfi, and stopped for lunch. The driver went off by himself with the thousand lire Merrick gave him for his meal, and Merrick lunched at a hotel whose dining terrace overlooked the sea. He had been here for lunch or dinner a couple of times with Helena, but he did not dwell on that as he slowly ate the good meal. He found that being in Amalfi did not trouble him. Why should it? The very hotel where he and she had stayed had been destroyed one winter in a landslide caused by heavy rains. They had built it back, of course, and in the former style, Merrick had heard, but he was sure this was not quite true. There would have been a few changes, probably in the direction of enlargement, and they could not have recovered every rock and stone and tree. But if the hotel had remained exactly the same, Merrick would not have gone to it now. He knew that his own memory in twenty-five years must have undergone slow changes, and that reality would be a shock, useless and depressing.

Merrick lingered over his lunch, then had a leisurely coffee and brandy down on the main plaza. It was nearly five before they went on.

The next town of any size was Positano. It was the end of the day, and a huge orange sun was just dropping into the sea beyond the purple hump of Capri. Merrick imagined that he had heard the sun hiss as it touched the water, but the hiss was the lappings of waves against the rocky cliffs below. Positano, though objectively beautiful set in its curve of mountains – like the banked benches of an amphitheatre whose stage was the flat sea in front – looked no more inviting to Merrick than a half dozen other villages he had seen. Still, he told the driver that he would stay here for the night. The driver was quite surprised, because Merrick had told him they might drive to Naples and even to Rome. Merrick said he would pay him what he would have paid him to go to Rome, and this pleased the driver.

'I know the best hotel here, sir. Shall I take you there?'

Merrick did not want to come to a decision so soon. 'No. Drive through the town first. Please.'

The road took them above the town, round the semicircle of the amphitheatre. There were no roads in the town proper, only steps and slanting footpaths.

'What about this?' Merrick said, indicating a hotel on their left. Its wrought-iron sign said Hotel Orlando, flat and black against its white front.

'Very well.' The driver pulled into the parking area in front of the hotel.

A bellboy came out.

It was probably a very ordinary hotel, Merrick thought, but it looked rather expensive, so he supposed it would be clean and the service good. Merrick paid the driver and tipped him.

Merrick undressed in his room and had a slow, hot bath. Then he put on his dressing-gown and ordered a half bottle of champagne to be sent to his room. With the cheer of the champagne, he forced himself to write a postcard to his sister in New

York and to his daughter-in-law, both of whom were worried about him. To both he wrote the same thing:

Having a very enjoyable time, resting as prescribed. Joining the Denises in Munich soon. Hope you are well. Don't worry. Much love,
Charles

His doctors had told him to rest for two hours in bed in the afternoons. Merrick had done this until Palermo, but not since, not for three days. Four months ago his wife Helena and their only son, their only child, Adam, had been killed in a collision on a New Jersey parkway in a car driven by Adam. Merrick had not reacted badly at first, but he had three months later. He had had to stop going to his office at Merrick Weaves, Inc. in White Plains, not really because he felt as bad as the doctors thought he did, but because his going seemed to have no purpose. The textile factory continued to produce just as well without him as with him. His sister Wynne had come to stay in his White Plains house with him for two weeks, but since she had a household of her own, that couldn't last for ever. Her presence in the empty house, wonderful as Wynne was, had really not touched Merrick's melancholia, anyway, though he had pretended to her that he felt better. He lost weight even though it seemed to him, perhaps because of the effort it took, that he was poking the same amount of food down himself as he always had. He had not realized that he loved Helena so much, that he so needed her simply to exist. The loss of her plus his son just out of college, just finished his military service, just married, just ready to start living – had been enough to shake his faith in everything he had lived by until then. The virtues of hard work, honesty, respect for one's fellow man, belief in God, had seemed suddenly so thin and abstract. His convictions had become ghostlike, whereas the bodies of his wife and son in the funeral chapel had been as tangible as stone. The emptiness of his home had been real, but not the abstract ideal of manly fortitude. At the same time, Merrick knew that millions of men had been here before, since the beginning of time. There was nothing unusual or original about his feelings. It was what people called 'life' – the two deaths in his life, and their aftermath. Finally his doctors had recommended a leisurely trip to Europe, but before endorsing this prescription had made sure that Merrick planned to see friends in London, Paris, Rome and Munich, and that the friends were the kind who would have time to spend with him. Though his boat went to Genoa, Merrick had abandoned it in Lisbon, its first port, and had taken another boat to Palermo. The Martins in Rome wanted him to stay with them for a week in their large house on the Via Appia Antica. Merrick hoped to make that an overnight stay, on the excuse that the Denises were expecting him in Munich earlier than he had thought. The Denises lived in Zurich and were coming to Munich especially to join him. From Munich, they were to drive down to Venice, then into Yugoslavia and down its coast.

Dinner was served at eight, Merrick had been told. At seven-thirty, he wandered into the garden behind the terrace where all the tables were set for dinner. The garden was dimly lighted by a few candles in glasses set along the low stone wall and on nearly buried stones in the grass. It was a wild garden, if one could call it a garden at all, but as soon as Merrick saw it, he was entranced. There was a swing chair on the left, half hidden by a low tree, where two people sat, a small table in front of them with drinks on it. There was no one else in the garden. Far behind, black now since the sun had gone down, rose the forms of huge mountains that seemed very close, walling the garden in. The candlelight lit up the faces of the couple in the swing chair like the faces of children around a lighted Hallowe'en pumpkin. Perhaps they were newlyweds, Merrick thought. Something about them suggested it, not their physical closeness because they were not even touching each other, but their quiet happiness and familiarity, their youth.

A guitar began to play. It seemed to come from below, where the ground fell in dark clumps of bush and tree – though there was nothing down there, no light. The guitar was unaccompanied, yet it had the richness of three instruments playing together. The song glided in an easy, self-confident manner. Its melody line was long and intricate, down to a bass note that seemed to vibrate in Merrick's blood when the player came to it now and again. He realized it was probably only a popular slow foxtrot, yet now it seemed far better, almost like an aria destined to be famous, from an opera by a great composer. Merrick took a deep breath. There had been such a song in Amalfi when he and Helena had been there. He had never heard the song since, and he and Helena had never taken the trouble to find out its name or to buy a record of it to take back to the States. It had simply been played, on a guitar also, now and then in the evening at their hotel. They had known it would turn up, like a certain bird at sunset, sometimes, and it would not have been fitting to ask its name, to ask a musician to play it for them, because it had its own times of turning up.

At dinner, Merrick had a table, which might have seated four, to himself, set against a decorative rail of the terrace. Bougainvillaea grew up from below and climbed the rail, so close that a pale purple clump of it could lie on the white tablecloth beside his right hand. Merrick looked around at his fellow diners. There were more young people than old. He saw the newlyweds, still engrossed in each other and talking, at a table in the centre of the terrace. In the far corner sat a middle-aged woman with light-brown hair, a very well-dressed woman who looked American, eating by herself. Merrick blinked and stared at her, then at the corner – less than a right angle – made by the terrace and the rail behind her. It was exactly like a certain corner of the terrace in the hotel in Amalfi. There had been bougainvillaea there, too. But the rest of the hotel was not like the hotel in Amalfi, not like it, and yet just enough like it. There had been, for instance, a garden left in a state of nature in the Amalfi hotel, like this one. Then Merrick realized he had at last come to the right place.

'Finished, *signor*?'

Merrick's antipasto plate was taken away, and the smiling Italian waiter, who looked no more than sixteen, held a large tray of *fettucini* for him to help himself. This was followed by roast veal, a green salad, then a large basket of fruit, from which Merrick chose a pear, then a sweet. Merrick ordered coffee served to him in the garden, and he drank it standing at the garden rail, though there was no one now in the swing seat or in the two deck chairs near it.

The woman with the light-brown hair and small pendant ear-rings came into the garden, and bent her head to light her cigarette. Her lighter only sparked.

'Allow me?' said Merrick, coming toward her, pulling his lighter out of his jacket with his free hand.

'Oh! – I didn't see anybody there. Thank you.'

She was not in the least like Helena, though when he had seen her sitting in the corner of the terrace, he had thought she was – like Helena as she might have looked today, if she had sat in the corner of the Amalfi hotel terrace.

'You've just arrived, haven't you?' said the woman pleasantly. Her blue eyes had little crinkles of lines around them. Her face was suntanned.

'Yes. You've been here a long while?'

'Five weeks. I come here every year. I paint at the art school. Mostly as a hobby, you know. You must come and see our school. Come before twelve-thirty, because it closes then, then we all go down to have lunch on the beach.'

Merrick made a little bow. 'Thank you. I would like to.' He hesitated, then drifted away.

The next morning, he passed the art school, which was in an old palace with huge doors that stood open to an inner loggia and court, but he did not go in. He went down and stared at the water and the bathers for a while, bought the New York and the London *Times* at the newspaper store, and while he was sitting on the low cement parapet above the beach reading them, a small boy came up and asked him if he would like a shine.

Merrick looked at him and smiled with amusement. 'A shine? For these shoes?' Merrick was wearing dark-blue espadrilles.

The boy was grinning, too. His pale-blue trousers were dirty and had a patch on one knee. 'I can ask, can't I?'

'And you haven't any equipment,' Merrick said. 'Where's your polish?'

'Here,' the boy said, slapping a pocket that obviously contained nothing. 'Fifty lire. Cheap.'

Merrick laughed. 'I'll buy you an ice-cream cone. Here – ' He pulled his change out of his pocket. 'Here's fifty lire.' Merrick got up as if motivated by some force not his own. 'Let's get an ice-cream cone.'

They went to the *gelateria* on the beach front, the boy skipping in circles about Merrick as if Merrick were some captive he was throwing invisible ropes around. Merrick bought him a double chocolate cone. It put a wide border of sticky brown around the boy's mouth.

'Where are you from in America? . . . Why are you here? . . . How long are you staying? . . . Have you got a car? . . . Have you got a boat? . . . Have you got a wife? . . . Have you got a big house in America? . . . How old are you?'

Merrick answered all his questions honestly, without restraint, smiling, even to the 'No' that he said when the boy asked if he had a wife.

The boy accompanied him to the post office, where he had to post an airmail letter to Merrick Weaves, then walked on up the road with him toward his hotel. Merrick was charmed by his naturalness, his utter lack of inhibition – the boy paused by the roadside to urinate, not even stepping behind a tree – and he almost invited the boy into the hotel. He could have ordered iced lemonade and cake as a treat. But Merrick thought it was probably not the thing to do. He wished he could be as free as the child. The boy made Merrick think of a small puppy with the miraculous ability to talk.

That evening Merrick was more than ever delighted with the Hotel Orlando. The guitar played the wonderful song again.

Merrick was so lost in his dreams of Helena, he scarcely heard the few remarks of the waiter, and only replied by gestures. He had coffee at the table.

'Good evening! We're playing bridge in the lounge tonight, and I wonder if you'd like to join us? Just myself and Mr and Mrs Gifford. Have you met them?' It was the woman with the light-brown hair again.

Merrick looked at her as though she were a thousand miles away instead of right by his table. Her voice had even sounded faint, and now, suddenly, he could not even remember what she had said. At last, he got to his feet. 'Good evening, I – '

'You're not sick?'

'No.'

'Good. So many people do get sick here at first.' She smiled.

'I did go by the art school, but I didn't go in,' Merrick said, thinking she had said something about the school.

'Oh. Well, any time for that. What about bridge?'

Merrick suddenly saw the suicide on the bridge, all over again, and again pulled his hand down his face. 'No, thank you. I don't like it,' he said gently.

The woman's face looked surprised. 'All right. Never mind. Sorry.' With a faint smile she was gone.

The next day, Merrick did not leave the hotel until afternoon. The small boy was on the beach front again, standing and chatting with a young couple who looked English, but when he saw Merrick, he detached himself with a wave of his hand to the couple, and came running.

'Hello! How are you today? . . . What have you been doing? . . . Why weren't you here this morning . . . How much did your shirt cost? . . . Were you *born* in America?'

They walked along the beach, picking up interesting pebbles and fragments of coloured tiles, worn smooth by the water. The boy chatted with some fishermen who were sitting on the sand mending long, rust-coloured nets. The fishermen called him Seppe or Guiseppe, and laughed and winked at Merrick as they talked with him. Merrick could understand little of what they said, because it was all in dialect. Seppe was barefoot and thin, but in his eyes and his laughing mouth, Merrick saw the vitality of a people that poverty could never crush. Merrick thought of the suicide Bartucci's children, knew the same vitality would be in them, though perhaps not now the laughter. He decided to send the widow some money. He remembered the name of the town to the south where she lived. He could send a money order, anonymously. This thought made him feel happy.

'Seppe,' he said as they walked on past the net-menders. 'Would you like to have dinner with me in my hotel tonight?'

'Ah-h-h!' Seppe stopped, crouched with his hands in an attitude of prayer, and beamed up at Merrick. '*Momma mia, si!*'

'But you've got to be quiet at dinner. And maybe you have some cleaner pants?'

'Ah, *si!* I've got a real suit at home!'

'Wear it. Dinner is at eight. Not too late for you?'

'*Late?*' Seppe said, insulted, laughing.

That evening, Merrick was by the steps of the hotel at seven-thirty, fearing that Seppe would be early. He was. He was wearing his suit, new and brown and too big for him, but his shoes were worn and needed a shine. His wetted black hair showed the marks of a comb.

'Hello!' the boy called loudly to Merrick, but his eyes darted everywhere else, taking in the splendour.

'Hello,' Merrick said. 'We have time for a lemonade or something. Let's go in the garden.'

They went into the garden. Merrick found a waiter and ordered one lemonade and one Cinzano. In the garden, the boy continued to chatter and peer at everything, but for once Merrick did not listen to him. Merrick lifted his head a little and listened to the guitar music, gazed at the tree-sheltered swing chair in which the newlyweds again sat, and he dreamed. The boy did not seem to mind. He drank his lemonade thirstily between his sentences.

At dinner, the boy ate heartily of everything, and had a glass of Merrick's wine. Seppe declared that he was going to be a hotel-keeper when he grew up. He accepted Merrick's offer of a second helping of dessert. Afterward, the boy put one hand over his stomach, closed his eyes and said, 'Oooooh,' but he was feeling very well. Merrick smoked over his coffee. They had taken long over dinner, and the terrace was almost deserted.

'Can I go to the toilet?' asked the boy.

'Certainly. It's inside that door – ' Merrick pointed, got it wrong, shook his head, and pointed to the right door. 'You'll see a door saying *signori*. Not the *signore*.'

Seppe smiled and dashed away.

He was gone quite a while, Merrick thought, though he was not sure, and automatically looked at his watch, as if that could tell him anything, for he hadn't the slightest idea what time it had been when the boy left. Then just as Merrick turned around, the boy appeared, on his way back.

'Can I have a cigarette?' It was the second time Seppe had asked him.

'I'm afraid not,' Merrick said, refusing for the second time, though he felt himself relenting. Alone, he would have given the boy a cigarette. 'Why don't we take a little walk?'

They walked up the road that went past the hotel. Seppe was quieter, as if the darkness had muted him.

'Where do you live?' Merrick asked.

'Down there.' Seppe pointed behind him.

'We should walk that way then. It's late.' Merrick turned.

When they came to the Hotel Orlando again, Seppe waved a hand and said, 'I'll see you tomorrow on the beach. Good-bye!'

'Good-bye,' Merrick said.

'*Grazie!*'

'*Prego!*'

Merrick went into his hotel. As he crossed the lobby, the manager, a man of about forty with a moustache, came toward him.

'*Signor* Merrick – ah – ' He beckoned Merrick into a corner of the lobby. Before he could speak, a large-breasted blonde

Italian woman came up and joined them, saying to Merrick:

'*Signor,* excuse me, but we cannot take street boys into our hotel. Never!'

'Signor – Just a minute, Eleanora, *piano piano,* I will talk to him. First of all, we are not sure.'

'Ah-h, sure enough!' said Eleanora.

'Signor,' continued the manager, 'there has been a small robbery.'

Now the American woman with the light-brown hair was walking toward them. 'Hello. Look – I'm not trying to make any accusations, but my gold compact, my cigarette lighter – '

'And fifty thousand lire,' Eleanora put in.

'All I had in this bag,' said the American woman, holding out a tapestry bag to show Merrick. 'I didn't miss anything till two minutes ago. The only time it was out of my sight was when I had it on the table in the ladies' room for two minutes.'

'A clever thief. He put rocks in it to weight it,' said Eleanora. 'Show them.'

'Yes,' said the American woman, smiling a little. 'Stones from the beach.'

Merrick looked into her open pocketbook and saw some broken tiles of the sort he and Seppe had gathered that afternoon.

'Did that street boy leave you this evening to go to the toilet?' asked Eleanora. 'He did. I saw him leave the table. That boy, I know him, I know his face. He is not a good boy. They call him Seppe. What is his last name?' She frowned as if the name would come to her, and looked at the manager. Then to Merrick, 'Where does he live?'

'I don't know,' Merrick said, in a daze. 'I am sure he *didn't,*' he said earnestly.

But despite his conviction, Merrick was completely over-ridden. The manager went to the desk to call the police. The blonde Italian woman continued to rant about street boys in decent hotels, the American woman was downcast over her gold compact, but not angry at Merrick.

'I will certainly do what I can,' Merrick said. 'Certainly.' But he hadn't the least idea what to do.

Somehow, Merrick and the American woman found themselves out in the garden. Each was having a brandy. Merrick was jolted by its sharpness in his mouth. He tried to listen to what the woman was saying. But it seemed of no importance whatever. It seemed they were waiting for something. When Merrick finally looked at his watch, it was after midnight.

The hotel manager came out to tell them that the police had gone to the boy's house, but that the boy had not come home. 'His name is Dell' Isola. He lives up in Città Morta.' He waved an arm at another section of the town, which Merrick knew sat halfway up a mountain. '*Signora*, I am sorry. The morning should shed some light.' The manager smiled, and left.

The next thing Merrick was really conscious of was the hot water in his bath. He could not believe it. No, it was too absurd. The stones – they could have been put there by anybody. Certainly it was a clever action, the action of an old, experienced thief.

The next morning at nine, when Merrick came out of his room, the manager greeted him in the hall and said, 'Well, the boy is home this morning. He came in very late last night, his mother said. But of course they deny everything. No money, no compact, nothing. They are together, the whole family.' He waggled his hand, palm downward. 'The police searched the house, of course.'

'Well – you see?' Merrick replied calmly. 'I'm sorry it happened, but you see it wasn't Seppe.'

The manager's lips parted, but he did not say anything.

Merrick walked on. In the lobby, the desk clerk handed him a telegram that he said had just come in. It was from the Denises.

DON'T WORRY. YOU ARE AHEAD SCHEDULE. STILL IN
ZURICH. MUNICH SENT US TELEGRAM. SEE YOU SOON
MUNICH. LOVE. BETTY-ALEX

He must have wired them that he would be late for Munich, Merrick realized. But when had he sent the wire? He didn't remember sending it. He only remembered feeling intensely a couple of days ago that he must stay on and on at the Orlando, and that he didn't want any engagements to pry him away.

Merrick stopped at the small bank of the town and cashed two thousand dollars in Travellers Cheques into lire. Then he took the lire to the post office and made out four money orders for lire to the equivalent of five hundred dollars each, and sent them to Mrs Dino Bartucci in the little town.

Seppe was not down at the beach that morning. Merrick lunched at a beach front restaurant and around two, he saw Seppe hopping down the plaza steps on one bare foot, his hands in his pockets. Then he whirled in circles, his eyes shut, like a blind dancer. From these antics, Merrick knew that Seppe had seen him, no doubt before Merrick saw him. At last Seppe drifted over, hands still in his pockets, and with a timid smile.

'Well, good afternoon,' said Merrick.

'Hi.'

'I hear the police called on you last night. This morning, too.'

'Yes, but they didn't find anything. Why should they?' His hands flew out. 'I didn't have anything.' Seppe's eyes were earnest and intense.

Merrick smiled and relaxed. 'No, I didn't think you did.'

'*Gesu Maria*! Poilice in *my* house!' He glanced around to see if anyone were listening, though he had not spoken loudly, and the man at the nearest table was buried behind the Paris *Herald-Tribune*. 'I never had police in *my* house before. What did you tell them?'

'Well – I certainly didn't tell them to go looking for you. It was the hotel manager's idea. Sit down, Seppe. – They thought you robbed a woman's pocketbook. I couldn't stop them from going to you.'

Seppe said something under his breath that Merrick could not understand, and shook his head.

'I've just had lunch. Would you like something?'

They spent the afternoon together, taking a carozza ride around the town, and shooting rifles at a booth in a corner of the plaza. But Seppe did not walk all the way back to the hotel with Merrick. He stopped at the last curve in the road before the hotel, and said with an air of contempt (for the hotel) that he didn't care to walk any farther.

'Okay,' Merrick said agreeably. 'Well – take it easy, Seppe. See you tomorrow maybe.' He went on.

The woman who had been robbed did not speak to Merrick that evening, or even nod to him. Merrick didn't care. She associated him with her loss, mistakenly, and there was nothing he could do about it. Merrick sat long in the swing chair after dinner, alone and dreaming.

Seppe seemed much happier the next day, and also the day after that, when he announced that his father was going to buy a television set.

Merrick looked at Seppe and thought, *could* it be that he had stolen all those lire, the compact? Merrick frowned. No. His whole mind and his heart rejected the idea. 'Seppe, you did not take the money from the lady's pocketbook – did you?'

They were leaning against an inverted fishing boat on the beach.

'No,' Seppe said, but less positively than three days before.

Merrick frowned harder, and forced himself to say, 'I'll give you – ten thousand lire if you tell me the truth.'

Seppe grinned mischievously. 'Let's see the ten thousand.'

'Tell me the truth first.'

'All right. I stole it,' he said softly.

Merrick began to breathe shallowly, as if a weight sat on his chest. *I don't believe you*, he thought. And he made no move to reach for the lire.

'Where is the ten thousand?'

'I don't believe you. Prove that you stole it.'

'Prove it?' The mischievous grin grew wider. Seppe pulled a hand slowly from his pocket, and looked around him as the hand came out in a fist. The fist opened, and in his palm lay a lipstick which looked like gold, but wasn't, Merrick knew, though it was obviously expensive. It was set with small red stones that sparkled like cut rubies. The lipstick case seemed to scream that it was American, and the possession of the rich woman with the light-brown hair.

Merrick believed. He saw in a rush, Seppe spilling out his loot in his house, the fifty thousand lire being hidden somewhere, the gold compact and the lighter whisked off by someone, maybe by an older brother, to be sold in Rome. Merrick ground his teeth and set them together. Then he walked away. He walked slowly. The boy came tagging after him, asking him questions in an anxious tone, pleading with him, hanging finally to Merrick's wrist, but Merrick paid no attention to him. Merrick walked on past the place where people turned to go into the town. He walked on along the beach, and finally Seppe unstuck himself and hung back and Merrick was alone.

That night, Merrick sat so long in the garden that a busboy, come to collect the glasses of the candles that had burned out, told him that they were about to close the gates. Merrick detested walking into the hotel hall, into his room. It was like living the naked, painful moment all over again, when he had learned that Seppe had stolen.

Merrick received in the morning post his four money orders with their envelopes unopened. On each one was stamped DEFUNTO, the Italian word for deceased. They had mistaken *Signora* for *Signor,* Merrick thought, though on each envelope, *Signora* was clearly spelled out. Merrick went straight to the post office with the envelopes.

'Ah, *si*,' said the woman behind the money order window. 'We noticed these this morning . . . No, it is not a mistake, the wife is dead also.' She turned around. 'Franco! Come here a moment.'

A dark-haired young man in shirtsleeves came over, glanced at the envelopes and said, 'Ah, *si!*' then looked at Merrick. '*Si signor*, I happen to know, because I have a cousin who lives in that town. The mother killed herself and her five children

139

with gas from the oven. Just two or three days ago.'

Merrick was stunned. 'You're sure?'

'Sure, *signor*. *Sicuro*. The *defunto* was stamped in the village. Besides, my cousin wrote me.'

'Thank you.' Merrick gathered his envelopes together. One, two, three, four. Each seemed to be a slap in his face.

'*Signor!* — You must cash them,' said the woman at the window, and Merrick turned back. 'What can you do with them?' she asked rhetorically, with a smile and a shrug. 'You knew the woman, too?'

Merrick shook his head. 'No.'

Five minutes later, he walked out of the post office with a piece of paper that would enable him to get the money from the town bank. He went back to the hotel and sat in the garden. He missed lunch, and only reluctantly left the garden around eight to bathe and then to have dinner. That night, he told the busboy that he wished to spend the night in the garden, whether they locked the gate or not.

'It becomes cold, sir,' said the boy.

'Not very cold.'

It became cold toward dawn, but Merrick did not mind it. He changed his clothes early in the morning for slacks and a sport-shirt, then returned to the garden with a book, which he did not read. Only in the garden did he feel secure, as if he had a grasp of any kind on life or his own existence. Though he was quite aware that Helena was not with him, in the flesh, she was with him every other way in the garden. He did not have any illusions of hearing her voice, it was not so physical, what he felt, but he felt her presence in every particle of the air, in every blade of grass, every flower, bush and tree. She loved the garden as much as he. His thoughts were also unphysical, never of Helena's smile, but of her good nature, of her wonderful health that had let her ride horseback, play tennis and swim right up to the time of her death, of her love and her care for their home, whatever and wherever it had been — a simple home at first, yet even when they had acquired a staff of servants, Helena had never stopped doing some of the cooking: every dinner had to have some item in it that she had prepared with her own hands.

The blonde Italian woman whose name Merrick had forgotten came out to speak to him.

'I'm quite comfortable here,' Merrick said. 'If I'm not bothering anyone else,' he added somewhat challengingly. He did not monopolize the swing chair, certainly, but frequently walked about or sat on a rock.

She said something about his health, catching a cold, and about his room being unsatisfactory.

'There's nothing wrong with my room, I prefer the garden,' Merrick said.

Some time later, it rained. Merrick sat in the swing chair, which had a short roof, but his feet and the lower part of his legs got soaked. He was oblivious of it, or rather he didn't mind. A garden could not for ever be a garden without rain. Two or three people ran out to speak to him during the rain, and ran back again, but when the rain stopped, five people came out, three who spoke to him and two who just stood and watched curiously.

'I don't see that I'm bothering anyone,' Merrick said. This was all he said, but even this seemed to bother them.

Finally, a single new man came out, and said he was a doctor. He sat on a chair and talked calmly to Merrick, but Merrick was not interested in anything he had to say.

'I prefer the garden,' Merrick said.

The man went away.

Merrick knew what would happen if he enjoyed the garden much longer, however, so after smoking a cigarette he got up, went into the lobby and asked for his bill. Then he sent a telegram of confirmation to the Denises about Munich. The next leg of the journey.

The Barbarians

Stanley Hubbell painted on Sundays, the only day he had to paint. Saturdays he helped his father in the hardware store in Brooklyn. Weekdays he worked as a researcher for a publishing house specializing in trade journals. Stanley did not take his painting very seriously: it was a kind of occupational therapy for his nerves recommended by his doctor. After six months, he was painting fairly well.

One Sunday in early June, Stanley was completing a portrait of himself in a white shirt with a green background. It was larger than his first self-portrait, and it was much better. He had caught the troubled frown of his left eyebrow. The eyes were finished – light brown, a little sad, intense, hopeful. Hopeful of what? Stanley didn't know. But the eyes on the canvas were so much his own eyes they made him smile with pleasure when he looked at them. There remained the highlight to put down the long, somewhat crooked nose, and then to darken the background.

He had been working perhaps twenty minutes, hardly long enough to moisten his brushes or limber up the colours on his palette, when he heard them stomping through the narrow alley at the side of his building. He hesitated, while half his mind still imagined the unpainted highlight down the nose and the other half listened to find out how many there were going to be this afternoon.

Do it now, he told himself, and quickly bent toward the canvas, his left hand clutching the canvas frame, his right hand braced against his left forearm. The point of his brush touched the bridge of his nose.

'Let's *have* it, Franky!'

'*Yee-hoool*'

'*Ah, g'wan! What dyuh think I wanna do? Fight the whole goddam . . .*'

'Ah-ha-*haaaaaaah*!'

'Put it *here*, Franky!'

Thud!

They always warmed up for fifteen minutes or so with a hard ball and catchers' mitts.

Stanley's brush stopped after half an inch. He paused, hoping for a lull, knowing there wouldn't be any. The braying voices went on, twenty feet below his window, bantering, directing one another, explaining, exhorting.

'*Get the goddamn bush outa the way! Pull it up!*' a voice yelled. Stanley flinched as if it had been said to him.

Two Sundays ago they had had quite an exchange about the bushes. One of the men had tumbled over them in reaching for the ball, and Stanley, seeing it, had shouted down: 'Would you please not go against the hedge?' It burst out of him involuntarily – he was sorry he had not made the remark a lot stronger – and they had all joined in yelling back at him: 'What d'yuh think this is, your lot?' and 'Who're you, the gardener? – Hedges! Hah!'

Stanley edged closer to the window, close enough to see the bottom of the brick wall that bounded the far side of the lot. There were still five little bushes standing in front of the wall, forlorn and scraggly, but still standing, still growing – at this minute. Stanley had put them there. He had found them growing, or rather struggling for surival, in cindery corners of the lot and by the ash-cans at the end of the alley. None of the bushes was more than two feet tall, but they were unmistakably hedge bushes. He had transplanted them for two reasons; to hide the ugly wall somewhat and to put the plants in a spot where they could get some sunshine. It had been a tiny gesture toward beautifying something that was, essentially, unbeautifiable, but he had made the effort and it had given him satisfaction. And the men seemed to know he had planted them, perhaps because he had shouted down to watch out for them, and also because the superintendent, who was never around and barely took care of the garbage cans, would never have done anything like set out hedge bushes by a brick wall.

Moving nearer the window, Stanley could see the men. There were five of them today, deployed around the narrow rectangular lot, throwing the ball to one another in no particular order, which meant that four were at all times yelling for the ball to be thrown to them.

'Here y'are Joey, *here!*'

Thud!

They were all men of thirty or more, and two had the beginnings of paunches. One of the paunchy men was red-headed and he had the loudest, most unpleasant voice, though it was the dark-haired man in blue jeans who yelled the most, really never stopped yelling, even when he caught and threw the ball, and by the same token none of his companions seemed to pay any attention to what he said. The redheaded man's name was Franky, Stanley had learned, and the dark-haired man was Bob. Two of the others had cleated shoes, and pranced and yelled between catches, lifting their knees high and pumping their arms.

'*Wanna see me break a window?*' yelled Franky, winding up. He slammed the ball at one of the cleat-shod men, who let out a wail as he caught it as if it had killed him.

Why was he watching it, Stanley asked himself. He looked at his clock. Only twenty past two. They would play until five, at least. Stanley was aware of a nervous trembling inside him, and he looked at his hands. They seemed absolutely steady. He walked to his canvas. The portrait looked like paint and canvas now, nothing more. The voices might have been in the same room with him. He went to one window and closed it. It was really too hot to close both windows.

Then, from somewhere above him, Stanley heard a window go up, and as if it were a signal for battle, he stiffened: the window-opener was on his side. Stanley stood a little back from the window and looked down at the lot.

'Hey!' the voice from upstairs cried. 'Don't you know you're not supposed to play ball there? People're trying to sleep!'

'*Go ahead'n sleep!*' yelled the blue jeans, spitting on the ground between his spread knees.

An obscenity from the redhead, and then, 'Let's go, Joey, let's *have* it!'

'Hey! – I'm going to get the law on you if you don't clear out!' from the upstairs window.

The old man was really angry – it was Mr Collins, the night-watchman – but the threat of the law was empty and every-body knew it. Stanley had spoken to a policeman a month ago, told him about the Sunday ballplayers, but the policeman had only smiled at him – a smile of indulgence for the ball-players – and had mumbled something about nobody's being able to do anything about people who wanted to play ball on Sundays. Why couldn't you, Stanley wondered. What about the NO BALLPLAYING written on the side of his own building and signed by the Police Department? What about the right of law-abiding citizens to spend a quiet Sunday at home if they cared to? What about the anti-noise campaign in New York? But he hadn't asked the policeman these questions, because he had seen that the policeman was the same kind of man the ball-players were, only in uniform.

They were still yelling, Mr Collins and the quintet below. Stanley put his palms on the brick ledge of the windowsill and leaned out to add the support of his visible presence to Mr Collins.

'*We ain't breakin' any law! Go to hell!*'

'I mean what I say!' shouted Mr Collins. 'I'm a working man!'

'*Go back to bed, grampa!*'

Then the redheaded man picked up a stone or a large cinder and made as if to throw it at Mr Collins, whose voice shut off in the middle of a sentence. '*Shut up or we'll bust yuh win-*

dows!' the redheaded man bellowed, then managed to catch the ball that was coming his way.

Another window went up, and Stanley was suddenly inspired to yell: 'Isn't there another place to play ball around here? Can't you give us a break one Sunday?'

'Ah, the hell with 'em!' said one of the men.

The batted ball made a sick sound and spun up behind the batter, stopping in mid-air hardly four feet in front of Stanley's nose, before it started its descent. They were playing two-base baseball now with a stick bat and a soft ball.

The blonde woman who lived on the floor above Stanley and to the left was having a sympathetic discussion with Mr Collins: 'Wouldn't you think that grown men –'

Mr Collins, loudly: 'Ah, they're worse than children! Hoodlums, that's what they are! Ought to get the police after them!'

'And the language they use!·I've told my husband about 'em but he works Sundays and he just can't *realize!*'

'So her husband ain't home, huh?' said the redheaded man, and the others guffawed.

Stanley looked down on the bent, freckled back of the redheaded man who had removed his shirt now and whose hands were braced on his knees. It was a revolting sight – the white back mottled with brown freckles, rounded with fatty muscle and faintly shiny with sweat. I wish I had a BB gun, Stanley thought as he had often thought before. I'd shoot them, not enough to hurt them, just enough to annoy them. Annoy them the hell out of here!

A roar from five throats shocked him, shattered his thoughts and left him shaking.

He went into the bathroom and wet his face at the basin. Then he came back and closed his other window. The closed windows made very little difference in the sound. He bent toward his easel again, touching the brushtip to the partly drawn highlight on the nose. The tip of his brush had dried and stiffened. He moistened it in the turpentine cup.

'Frankyl'

'Run, boy run!'

Stanley put the brush down. He had made a wide white mark on the nose. He wiped at it with a rag, trembling.

Now there was an uproar from below, as if all five were fighting. Stanley looked out. Frank and the other pot-bellied man were wrestling for the ball by the hedges. With a wild, almost feminine laugh, the redhead toppled on to the hedges, yelping as the bushes scratched him.

Stanley flung the window up. 'Would you please watch out for the hedge?' he shouted.

'Ah, f'Chris' sake!' yelled the redhead, getting up from one knee, at the same time yanking up a bush from the ground and hurling it in Stanley's direction.

The others laughed.

'You're not allowed to destroy public property!' Stanley retorted with a quick, bitter smile, as if he had them. His heart was racing.

'What d'yuh mean we're not allowed?' asked the blue jeans, crashing a foot into another bush.

'Cut that out!' Stanley yelled.

'Oh, pipe down!'

'I'm gettin' thirsty! Who's goin' for drinks?'

Now the redhead man swung a foot and kicked another bush up into the air.

'Pick that hedge up again! Put it back!' Stanley shouted, clenching his fists.

'Pick up yer ass!'

Stanley crossed his room and yanked the door open, ran down the steps and out. Suddenly, he was standing in the middle of the lot in the bright sunshine. 'You'd better put that hedge back!' Stanley yelled. 'One of you'd better put all those bushes back!'

'Look who's here!'

'Oh, dry up! Come on, Joey!'

The ball hit Stanley on the shoulder, but he barely felt it, barely wondered if it had been directed at him. He was no match for any of the men physically, certainly not for all of them together, but this fact barely brushed the surface of his mind, either. He was mad enough to have attacked any or all of them, and it was only their scattered number that kept him from moving. He didn't know where to begin.

'Isn't any of you going to put those back?' he demanded. '*No!*'

'Outa the way, Mac! You're gonna get hurt!'

While reaching for the ball near Stanley, the blue jeans put out an arm and shoved him. Stanley's neck made a snapping sound and he just managed to recover his balance without pitching on his face. No one was paying the least attention to him now. They were like a scattered, mobile army, confident of their ground. Stanley walked quickly toward the alley, oblivious of the laughter that followed.

The next thing he knew, he was in the cool, darkish hall of his building. His eye fell on the flat stone that was used now and then to prop the front door open. He picked it up and began to climb the stairs with it. He thought of hurling it out his window, down into the midst of them. The barbarians!

He rested the stone on his windowsill, still holding it between his hands. The man in blue jeans was walking along by the brick wall, kicking at the remaining bushes. They had stopped playing for some reason.

'Got the stuff, fellows! Come 'n get it!' One of the pot-bellied men had arrived with his fists full of soft drink bottles.

Heads tipped back as they drank. There were animal murmers and grunts of satisfaction. Stanley leaned farther out.

The redheaded man was sitting right below his window on a board propped up on a couple of rocks to make a bench. He couldn't miss if he dropped it, Stanley thought, and almost at the same time, he held the stone a few inches out from his sill and dropped it. Ducking back, Stanley heard a deep-pitched, lethal-sounding crack, then a startled curse.

'Who did that?'

'Hey, Franky! *Franky!* Are you okay?'

Stanley heard a groan.

'We gotta get a doctor! Gimme a hand, somebody!'

'That bastard upstairs!' It came clearly.

Stanley jumped as something crashed through his other window, hit the shade and slid to the floor — a stone the size of a large egg.

Now he could hear their voices moving up the alley. Stanley expected them to come up the stairs for him. He clenched his fists and listened for feet on the stairs.

But nothing happened. Suddenly there was silence.

'Thank — *God*,' Stanley heard the blonde woman say, wearily.

The telephone would ring, he thought. That would be next. The police.

Stanley sat down in a chair, sat rigidly for several minutes. The rock had weighed eight or ten pounds, he thought. The very least that could have happened was that the man had suffered a concussion. But Stanley imagined the skull fractured, the brain partly crushed. Perhaps he had lived only a few moments after the impact.

He got up and went to his canvas. Boldly, he mixed a colour for the entire nose, painted over the messy highlight, then attacked the background, making it a darker green. By the time he had finished the background, the nose was dry enough for him to put the highlight in, which he did quickly and surely. There was no sound anywhere except that of his rather accelerated breathing. He painted as if he had only five minutes more to paint, five minutes more to live before they came for him.

But by six o'clock, nobody had come. The telephone had not rung, and the picture was done. It was good, better than he had dared hope it would be. Stanley felt exhausted. He remembered that there was no coffee in the house. No milk, either. He'd have to have a little coffee. He'd have to go out.

Fear was sneaking up on him again. Were they waiting for him downstairs in front of the house? Or were they still at the hospital, watching their friend die? What if he were dead?

You wouldn't kill a man for playing ball below your window on Sunday – even though you might like to.

He tried to pull himself together, went into the bathroom and took a quick, cool shower, because he had been perspiring quite a bit. He put on a clean blue shirt and combed his hair. Then he pushed his wallet and keys into his pocket and went out. He saw no sign of the ball-players on the sidewalk, or of anyone who seemed to be interested in him. He bought milk and coffee at the delicatessen around the corner, and on the way back he ran into the blonde woman of about forty who lived on the floor above him.

'Wasn't that awful this afternoon!' she said to Stanley. 'I saw you down there arguing with them. Good for you! You certainly scared them off.' She shook her head despairingly. 'But I suppose they'll be back next Sunday.'

'Do they play Saturdays?' Stanley asked suddenly, and entirely out of nervousness, since he didn't care whether they played Saturdays or not.

'No,' she said dubiously. 'Well, they once did, but mostly it's Sundays. I swear to God I'm going to make Al stay home one Sunday so he can hear 'em. You must have it a little worse than me, being lower down.' She shook her head again. She looked thin and tired, and there was a complicated meshwork of wrinkles under her lower lids. 'Well, you've got my thanks for breakin' 'em up a little earlier today.'

'Thank you,' Stanley said, really saying it almost involuntarily to thank her for not mentioning, for not having seen what he had done.

They climbed the stairs together.

'Trust this super not to be around whenever somebody needs him,' she said, loud enough to carry into the superintendent's second-floor apartment, which they were then passing. 'And to think we all give him big tips on Christmas!'

'It's pretty bad,' Stanley said with a smile as he unlocked his door. 'Well, let's hope next week's a little better.'

'You said it. I hope it's pouring rain,' she said, and went on up the stairs.

Stanley was in the habit of breakfasting at a small café between his house and the subway, and on Monday morning one of the ballplayers – the one who usually wore blue jeans – was in the café. He was having coffee and doughnuts when Stanley walked in, and he gave Stanley such an unpleasant look, continued for several minutes to give him such an unpleasant look, that a few other people in the café noticed it and began to watch them. Stanley stammeringly ordered coffee. The redheaded man wasn't dead, he decided. He was probably hovering between life and death. If Franky were dead, or if he were perfectly all right now, the dark-haired man's expression would have been different. Stanley finished his coffee and passed the man on the way to pay his check. He expected the man to try to trip him, or at least to say something to him as he passed him, but he didn't.

That evening, when Stanley came home from work at a little after six, he saw two of the ballplayers – the dark-haired man again and one of the paunchy men who looked like a wrestler in his ordinary clothes – standing across the street. They stared at him as he went into his building. Upstairs in his apartment, Stanley pondered the possible significance of their standing across the street from where he lived. Had their friend just died, or was he nearer death? Had they just come from the funeral, perhaps? Both of them had been wearing dark suits, suits that might have been their best. Stanley listened for feet on the stairs. There was only the plodding tread of the old woman who lived with her dog on the top floor. She aired her dog at about this time every evening.

All at once Stanley noticed that his windows were shattered. Now he saw three or four stones and fragments of glass on the carpet. There was a stone on his bed, too. The window that had been broken Sunday had almost no glass in it now, and of the upper halves of the windows, which were panelled, only two or three panels remained, he saw when he raised the shades.

He set about methodically picking up the stones and the larger pieces of glass and putting them into a paper bag. Then he got his broom and swept. He was wondering when he would have the time to put the glass back – no use asking the super to do it – and he thought probably not before next weekend, unless he ordered the pieces during his lunch hour tomorrow. He got his yardstick and measured the larger panes, which were of slightly different sizes because it was an old house, and then the panels, and recorded the numbers on a paper which he put into his wallet. He'd have to buy putty, too.

He stiffened, hearing a faint click at his doorlock. 'Who's there?' he called.

Silence.

He had an impulse to yank the door open, then realized he was afraid to. He listened for a few moments. There was no other sound, so he decided to forget the click. Maybe he had only imagined it.

When he came home the next evening he couldn't get his door open. The key went in, but it wouldn't turn, not a fraction of an inch. Had they put something in it to jam it? Had that been the click he had heard last night? On the other hand, the lock had given him some trouble about six months ago, he remembered. For several days it had been difficult to open, and then it had got all right again. Or had that been the lock on his father's store door? He couldn't quite remember.

He leaned against the stair rail, staring at the key in the lock and wondering what to do.

The blonde woman was coming up the stairs.

Stanley smiled and said. 'Good evening.'

'Hello, there. What happened? Forget your key?'

'No, I – The lock's a little stiff,' he said.

'Oh. Always something wrong in this house, ain't there?' she said, moving on down the hall. 'Did you ever see anything like it?'

'No,' he agreed, smiling. But he looked after her anxiously. Usually, she stopped and chatted a little longer. Had she heard something about his dropping the rock? And she hadn't mentioned his broken windows, though she was home all day and had probably heard the noise.

Stanley turned and attacked the lock, turning the key with all his strength. The lock suddenly yielded. The door was open.

It took him until after midnight to get the panes in. And all the time he worked, he was conscious of the fact that the windows might be broken again when he got home tomorrow.

The following evening the same two men, the paunchy one and the dark-haired one who was in blue jeans and a shirt now, were standing across the street, and to Stanley's horror they crossed the street so as to meet him in front of his door. The paunchy one reached out and took a handful of Stanley's jacket and shirtfront.

'Listen, Mac,' he said in Stanley's face, 'you can go to jail for what you did Sunday. You know that, doncha?'

'I don't know what you're talking about!' Stanley said quickly.

'Oh, you *don't*?'

'No!' Stanley yelled.

The man let him go with a shove. Stanley straightened his jacket, and went on into his house. The lock was again difficult, but he flung himself against it with the energy of desperation. It yielded slowly, and when Stanley removed his key, a rubbery string came with it: they had stuffed his lock with chewing gum. Stanley wiped his key, with disgust, on the floor. He did not begin to shake until he had closed the door of his apartment. Then even as he shook, he thought: I've beaten them. They weren't coming after him. Broken windows, chewing gum? So what? They hadn't sought out the police. He had lied, of course, in saying he didn't know what they were talking about, but that had been the right reply, after all. He wouldn't have lied to a policeman, naturally, but they hadn't brought the police in yet.

Stanley began to feel better. Moreover, his windows were intact, he saw. He decided that the redheaded man was probably going through a prolonged crisis. There was something subdued about the men's behaviour, he thought. Or were they planning some worse attack? He wished he knew if the redheaded man were in a hospital or walking around. It was just possible, too, that the man had died, Stanley thought. Maybe the men weren't quite sure that it was he who had dropped the rock – Mr Collins lived above Stanley and might have dropped it, for instance – and perhaps an investigation by the police was yet to come.

On Thursday evening, he passed Mr Collins on the stairs as he was coming home. Mr Collins was on his way to work. It struck Stanley that Mr Collins' 'Good evening' was cool. He wondered if Mr Collins had heard about the rock and considered him a murderer, or at least some kind of psychopath, to have dropped a ten-pound rock on somebody's head?

Saturday came, and Stanley worked all day in his father's hardware store, went to a movie, and came home at about eleven. Two of the small panes in the upper part of one window were broken. Stanley thought them not important enough to fix until the weather grew cooler. He wouldn't have noticed it, if he hadn't deliberately checked the state of the windows.

He slept late Sunday morning, for he had been extremely tired the night before. It was nearly one o'clock when he set up his easel to paint. He had in mind to paint the aperture between two buildings, which contained a tree, that he could see straight out his window above the lot. He thought this Sunday might be a good Sunday to paint, because the ballplayers probably wouldn't come. Stanley pictured them dampened this Sunday, at least to the extent that they would find another vacant lot to play in.

He had not quite finished his sketch of the scene in charcoal on his canvas, when he heard them. For a moment, he thought he was imagining it, that he was having an auditory hallucination. But no. He heard them ever more clearly in the alley – their particular sullen bravado coming through the murmuring, a collective murmur as recognizable to Stanley as a single familiar voice. Stanley waited, a little way back from the window.

'Okay, boys, let's *go-o-o*l'

'*Yeeeeee-hooooool*' Sheer defiance, a challenge to any who might contest their right to play there.

Stanley went closer to the window, looking, wide-eyed for the redheaded man. And there he was! A patch of bandage on the top of his head, but otherwise as brutishly energetic as ever. As Stanley watched, he hurled a catcher's mitt at a companion who was then bending over, hitting him in the buttocks.

Raucous, hooting laughter.

Then from above: 'F'gosh sakes, why don't you guys grow up? Why don't you beat it? We've had enough of you around here!' It was the blonde woman, and Stanley knew that Mr Collins would not be far behind.

'*Ah, save yer throat!*'

'C'mon down 'n get in the game, sister!'

There was a new defiance in their voices today. They were louder. They were determined to win. They *had* won. They were back.

Stanley sat down on his bed, dazed, frustrated, and suddenly tired. He was glad the redheaded fellow wasn't dead. He really was glad. And yet with his relief something fighting and bitter rose up in him, something borne on a wave of unshed tears.

'Let's have it, Joey, let's *have* it!'

Thud!

'Hey, Franky! Franky, look! Ah-ha-*haaaaaa*!'

Stanley put his hands over his ears, lifted his feet on to the bed, and shut his eyes. He lay in a Z position, his legs drawn up, and tried to be perfectly calm and quiet. No use fighting, he thought. No use fighting, no use crying.

Then he thought of something and sat up abruptly. He wished he had put the hedge bushes back. Now it was too late, he supposed, because they had been lying out on the ground for a week. But how he wished he had! Just that gesture of defiance, just that bit of beauty launched again in their faces.

The Empty Birdhouse

The first time Edith saw it she laughed, not believing her eyes.

She stepped to one side and looked again; it was still there, but a bit dimmer. A squirrel-like face – but demonic in its intensity – looked out at her from the round hole in the birdhouse. An illusion, of course, something to do with shadows, or a knot in the wood of the back wall of the birdhouse. The sunlight fell plain on the six-by-nine-inch birdhouse in the corner made by the toolshed and the brick wall of the garden. Edith went closer, until she was only ten feet away. The face disappeared.

That was funny, she thought, as she went back into the cottage. She would have to tell Charles tonight.

But she forgot to tell Charles.

Three days later she saw the face again. This time she was straightening up after having set two empty milk bottles on the back doorstep. A pair of beady black eyes looked out at her, straight and level, from the birdhouse, and they appeared to be surrounded by brownish fur. Edith flinched, then stood rigid. She thought she saw two rounded ears, a mouth that was neither animal nor bird, simply grim and cruel.

But she knew that the birdhouse was empty. The bluetit family had flown away weeks ago, and it had been a narrow squeak for the baby bluetits as the Masons' cat next door had been interested; the cat could reach the hole from the toolshed roof with a paw, and Charles had made the hole a trifle too big for bluetits. But Edith and Charles had staved Jonathan off until the birds were well away. Afterward, days later, Charles had taken the birdhouse down – it hung like a picture on a wire from a nail – and shaken it to make sure no debris was inside. Bluetits might nest a second time, he said. But they hadn't as yet – Edith was sure because she had kept watching.

And squirrels never nested in birdhouses. Or did they? At any rate, there were no squirrels around. Rats? They would never choose a birdhouse for a home. How could they get in, anyway, without flying?

While these thoughts went through Edith's mind, she started at the intense brown face, and the piercing black eyes stared back at her.

'I'll simply go and see what it is,' Edith thought, and stepped on to the path that led to the toolshed. But she went only three paces and stopped. She didn't want to touch the birdhouse and get bitten – maybe by a dirty rodent's tooth. She'd tell Charles tonight. But now that she was closer, the thing was still there, clearer than ever. It wasn't an optical illusion.

Her husband Charles Beaufort, a computing engineer, worked at a plant eight miles from where they lived. He frowned slightly and smiled when Edith told him what she had seen. 'Really?' he said.

'I *may* be wrong. I wish you'd shake the thing again and see if there's anything in it,' Edith said, smiling herself now, though her tone was earnest.

'All right, I will,' Charles said quickly, then began to talk of something else. They were then in the middle of dinner.

Edith had to remind him when they were putting the dishes into the dish-washing machine. She wanted him to look before it became dark. So Charles went out, and Edith stood on the doorstep, watching. Charles tapped on the birdhouse, listened with one ear cocked. He took the birdhouse down from the nail, shook it, then slowly tipped it so the hole was on the bottom. He shook it again.

'Absolutely nothing,' he called to Edith, 'Not even a piece of straw.' He smiled broadly at his wife and hung the birdhouse back on the nail. 'I wonder what you could've seen? You hadn't had a couple of Scotches, had you?'

'*No.* I described it to you.' Edith felt suddenly blank, deprived of something. 'It had a head a little larger than a squirrel's, beady black eyes, and a sort of serious mouth.'

'Serious mouth!' Charles put his head back and laughed as he came back into the house.

'A tense mouth. It had a grim look,' Edith said positively.

But she said nothing else about it. They sat in the living-room, Charles looking over the newspaper, then opening his folder of reports from the office. Edith had a catalogue and was trying to choose a tile pattern for the kitchen wall. Blue and white, or pink and white and blue? She was not in a mood to decide, and Charles was never a help, always saying agreeably, 'Whatever you like is all right with me.'

Edith was thirty-four. She and Charles had been married seven years. In the second year of their marriage Edith had lost the child she was carrying. She had lost it rather deliberately, being in a panic about giving birth. That was to say, her fall down the stairs had been rather on purpose, if she were willing to admit it, but the miscarriage had been put down as the result of an accident. She had never tried to have another child, and she and Charles had never even discussed it.

She considered herself and Charles a happy couple. Charles was doing well with Pan-Com Instruments, and they had more money and more freedom than several of their neighbours who were tied down with two or more children. They both liked entertaining, Edith in this house especially, and Charles on their boat, a thirty-foot motor launch which slept four. They plied the local river and inland canals on most weekends when the weather was good. Edith could cook almost as well afloat as on shore, and Charles obliged with drinks, fishing equipment, and the record player. He would also dance a hornpipe on request.

During the weekend that followed – not a boating weekend because Charles had extra work – Edith glanced several times at the empty birdhouse, reassured now because she *knew* there was nothing in it. When the sunlight shone on it she saw nothing but a paler brown in the round hole, the back of the birdhouse; and when in shadow the hole looked black.

On Monday afternoon, as she was changing the bedsheets in time for the laundryman who came at three, she saw something slip from under a blanket that she picked up from the floor. Something ran across the floor and out the door — something brown and larger than a squirrel. Edith gasped and dropped the blanket. She tiptoed to the bedroom door, looked into the hall and on the stairs, the first five steps of which she could see.

What kind of animal made no noise at all, even on bare wooden stairs? Or had she really seen anything? But she was sure she had. She'd even had a glimpse of the small black eyes. It was the same animal she had seen looking out of the birdhouse.

The only thing to do was to find it, she told herself. She thought at once of the hammer as a weapon in case of need, but the hammer was downstairs. She took a heavy book instead and went cautiously down the stairs, alert and looking everywhere as her vision widened at the foot of the stairs.

There was nothing in sight in the living-room. But it could be under the sofa or the armchair. She went into the kitchen and got the hammer from a drawer. Then she returned to the living-room and shoved the armchair quickly some three feet. Nothing. She found she was afraid to bend down to look under the sofa, whose cover came almost to the floor, but she pushed it a few inches and listened. Nothing.

It *might* have been a trick of her eyes, she supposed. Something like a spot floating before the eyes, after bending over the bed. She decided not to say anything to Charles about it. Yet in a way, what she had seen in the bedroom had been more definite than what she had seen in the birdhouse.

A baby yuma, she thought an hour later as she was sprinkling flour on a joint in the kitchen. A yuma. Now, where had that come from? Did such an animal exist? Had she seen a photograph of one in a magazine, or read the word somewhere?

Edith made herself finish all she intended to do in the kitchen, then went to the big dictionary and looked up the word yuma. It was not in the dictionary. A trick of her mind, she thought. Just as the animal was probably a trick of her eyes. But it was strange how they went together, as if the name was absolutely correct for the animal.

Two days later, as she and Charles were carrying their coffee cups into the kitchen, Edith saw it dart from under the refrigerator – or from behind the refrigerator – diagonally across the kitchen threshold and into the dining-room. She almost dropped her cup and saucer, but caught them, and they chattered in her hands.

'What's the matter?' Charles asked.

'I saw it again!' Edith said. 'The animal.'

'What?'

'I didn't tell you,' she began with a suddenly dry throat, as if she were making a painful confession. 'I think I saw that thing – the thing that was in the birdhouse – upstairs in the bedroom on Monday. And I think I saw it again. Just now.'

'Edith, my darling, there wasn't anything in the birdhouse.'

'Not when you looked. But this animal moves quickly. It almost flies.'

Charles's face grew more concerned. He looked where she was looking, at the kitchen threshold. 'You saw it just now? I'll go look,' he said, and walked into the dining-room.

He gazed around on the floor, glanced at his wife, then rather casually bent and looked under the table, among the chair legs. 'Really, Edith – '

'Look in the living-room,' Edith said.

Charles did, for perhaps fifteen seconds, then he came back, smiling a little. 'Sorry to say this, old girl, but I think you're seeing things. Unless, of course, it was a mouse. We might have mice. I hope not.'

'Oh, it's much bigger. And it's brown. Mice are grey.'

'Yep,' Charles said vaguely. 'Well, don't worry, dear, it's not going to attack you. It's running.' He added in a voice quite devoid of conviction, 'If necessary, we'll get an exterminator.'

'Yes,' she said at once.

'How big is it?'

She held her hands apart at a distance of about sixteen inches. 'This big.'

'Sounds like it might be a ferret,' he said.

'It's even quicker. And it has black eyes. Just now it stopped just for an instant and looked straight at me. Honestly, Charles.' Her voice had begun to shake. She pointed to the spot by the refrigerator. 'Just there it stopped for a split second and – '

'Edith, get a grip on yourself.' He pressed her arm.

'It looks so evil. I can't tell you.'

Charles was silent, looking at her.

'Is there any animal called a yuma?' she asked.

'A yuma? I've never heard of it. Why?'

'Because the name came to me today out of nowhere. I thought – because I'd thought of it and I'd never seen an animal like this that maybe I'd seen it somewhere.'

'Y-u-m-a?'

Edith nodded.

Charles, smiling again because it was turning into a funny game, went to the dictionary as Edith had done and looked for the word. He closed the dictionary and went to the *Encyclopaedia Britannica* on the bottom shelves of the bookcase. After a minute's search he said to Edith, 'Not in the dictionary and not in the *Britannica* either. I think it's a word you made up.' And he laughed. 'Or maybe it's a word in *Alice in Wonderland*.'

It's a real word, Edith thought, but she didn't have the courage to say so. Charles would deny it.

Edith felt done in and went to bed around ten with her book. But she was still reading when Charles came in just before eleven. At that moment both of them saw it: it flashed from the foot of the bed across the carpet, in plain view of Edith and Charles, went under the chest of drawers and, Edith thought, out the door. Charles must have thought so, too, as he turned quickly to look into the hall.

'You saw it!' Edith said.

Charles's face was stiff. He turned the light on in the hall, looked, then went down the stairs.

He was gone perhaps three minutes and Edith heard him pushing furniture about. Then he came back.

'Yes, I saw it.' His face looked suddenly pale and tired.

But Edith sighed and almost smiled, glad that he finally believed her. 'You see what I mean now. I wasn't seeing things.'

'No,' Charles agreed.

Edith was sitting up in bed. 'The awful thing is, it looks uncatchable.'

Charles began to unbutton his shirt. 'Uncatchable. What a word. Nothing's uncatchable. Maybe it's a ferret. Or a squirrel.'

'Couldn't you tell? It went right by you.'

'Well!' He laughed. 'It *was* pretty fast. You've seen it two or three times and you can't tell what it is.'

'Did it have a tail? I can't tell if it had or if that's the whole body – that length.'

Charles kept silent. He reached for his dressing gown, slowly put it on. 'I think it's smaller than it looks. It is fast, so it seems elongated. Might be a squirrel.'

'The eyes are in the front of its head. Squirrels' eyes are sort of at the side.'

Charles stooped at the foot of the bed and looked under it. He ran his hand over the tucked foot of the bed, underneath. Then he stood up. 'Look, if we see it again – *if* we saw it – '

'What do you mean *if*? You did see it – you said so.'

'I *think* so.' Charles laughed. 'How do I know my eyes or my mind isn't playing a trick on me? Your description was so eloquent.' He sounded almost angry with her.

'Well – *if*?'

'If we see it again, we'll borrow a cat. A cat'll find it.'

'Not the Masons' cat. I'd hate to ask them.'

They had had to throw pebbles at the Masons' cat to keep it away when the bluetits were starting to fly. The Masons hadn't liked that. They were still on good terms with the

Masons, but neither Edith nor Charles would have dreamed of asking to borrow Jonathan.

'We could call in an exterminator,' Edith said.

'Ha! And what'll we ask him to look for?'

'What we saw,' Edith said, annoyed because it was Charles who had suggested an exterminator just a couple of hours before. She was interested in the conversation, vitally interested, yet it depressed her. She felt it was vague and hopeless, and she wanted to lose herself in sleep.

'Let's try a cat,' Charles said. 'You know, Farrow has a cat. He got it from the people next door to him. You know, Farrow the accountant who lives on Shanley Road? He took the cat over when the people next door moved. But his wife doesn't like cats, he says. This one – '

'I'm not mad about cats either,' Edith said. 'We don't want to acquire a cat.'

'No. All right. But I'm sure we could borrow this one, and the reason I thought of it is that Farrow says the cat's a marvellous hunter. It's a female nine years old, he says.'

Charles came home with the cat the next evening, thirty minutes later than usual, because he had gone home with Farrow to fetch it. He and Edith closed the doors and the windows, then let the cat out of its basket in the living-room. The cat was white with grey brindle markings and black tail. She stood stiffly, looking all around her with a glum and somewhat disapproving air.

'Ther-re, Puss-Puss,' Charles said, stooping but not touching her. 'You're only going to be here a day or two. Have we got some milk, Edith? Or better yet, cream.'

They made a bed for the cat out of a carton, put an old towel in it, then placed it in a corner of the living-room, but the cat preferred the end of the sofa. She had explored the house perfunctorily and had shown no interest in the cupboards or closets, though Edith and Charles had hoped she would. Edith said she thought the cat was too old to be of much use in catching anything.

The next morning Mrs Farrow rang up Edith and told her

that they could keep Puss-Puss if they wanted to. 'She's a clean cat and very healthy. I just don't happen to like cats. So if you take to her – or she takes to you – '

Edith wriggled out by an unusually fluent burst of thanks and explanations of why they had borrowed the cat, and she promised to ring Mrs Farrow in a couple of days. Edith said she thought they had mice, but were not sure enough to call in an exterminator. This verbal effort exhausted her.

The cat spent most of her time sleeping either at the end of the sofa or on the foot of the bed upstairs, which Edith didn't care for but endured rather than alienate the cat. She even spoke affectionately to the cat and carried her to the open doors of closets, but Puss-Puss always stiffened slightly, not with fear but with boredom, and immediately turned away. Meanwhile she ate well of tuna, which the Farrows had prescribed.

Edith was polishing silver at the kitchen table on Friday afternoon when she saw the thing run straight beside her on the floor – from behind her, out the kitchen door into the dining-room like a brown rocket. And she saw it turn to the right into the living-room where the cat lay asleep.

Edith stood up at once and went to the living-room door. No sign of it now, and the cat's head still rested on her paws. The cat's eyes were closed. Edith's heart was beating fast. Her fear mingled with impatience and for an instant she experienced a sense of chaos and terrible disorder. The animal was in the room! And the cat was of no use at all! And the Wilsons were coming to dinner at seven o'clock. And she'd hardly have time to speak to Charles about it because he'd be washing and changing, and she couldn't, wouldn't mention it in front of the Wilsons, though they knew the Wilsons quite well. As Edith's chaos became frustration, tears burned her eyes. She imagined herself jumpy and awkward all evening, dropping things, and unable to say what was wrong.

'The yuma. The damned yuma!' she said softly and bitterly, then went back to the silver and doggedly finished polishing it and set the table.

The dinner, however, went quite well, and nothing was dropped or burned. Christopher Wilson and his wife Frances lived on the other side of the village, and had two boys, seven and five. Christopher was a lawyer for Pan-Com.

'You're looking a little peaked, Charles,' Christopher said. 'How about you and Edith joining us on Sunday?' He glanced at his wife. 'We're going for a swim at Hadden and then for a picnic. Just us and the kids. Lots of fresh air.'

'Oh – ' Charles waited for Edith to decline, but she was silent. 'Thanks very much. As for me – well, we'd thought of taking the boat somewhere. But we've borrowed a cat, and I don't think we should leave her alone all day.'

'A cat?' asked Frances Wilson. 'Borrowed it?'

'Yes. We thought we might have mice and wanted to find out,' Edith put in with a smile.

Frances asked a question or two about the cat and then the subject was dropped. Puss-Puss at that moment was upstairs, Edith thought. She always went upstairs when a new person came into the house.

Later when the Wilsons had left, Edith told Charles about seeing the animal again in the kitchen, and about the unconcern of Puss-Puss.

'That's the trouble. It doesn't make any noise,' Charles said. Then he frowned. 'Are you *sure* you saw it?'

'Just as sure as I am that I ever saw it,' Edith said.

'Let's give the cat a couple of more days,' Charles said.

The next morning, Saturday, Edith came downstairs around nine to start breakfast and stopped short at what she saw on the living-room floor. It was the yuma, dead, mangled at head and tail and abdomen. In fact, the tail was chewed off except for a damp stub about two inches long. And as for the head, there was none. But the fur was brown, almost black where it was damp with blood.

Edith turned and ran up the stairs.

'Charles!'

He was awake, but sleepy. 'What?'

'The cat caught it. It's in the living-room. Come down, will you? – I can't face it, I really can't.'

'Certainly, dear,' Charles said, throwing off the covers.

He was downstairs a few seconds later. Edith followed him.

'Um. Pretty big,' he said.

'What is it?'

'I dunno. I'll get the dustpan.' He went into the kitchen.

Edith hovered, watching him push it on to the dustpan with a rolled newspaper. He peered at the gore, a chewed windpipe, bones. The feet had little claws.

'What is it? A ferret?' Edith asked.

'I dunno. I really don't.' Charles wrapped the thing quickly in a newspaper. I'll get rid of it in the ashcan. Monday's garbage day, isn't it?'

Edith didn't answer.

Charles went through the kitchen and she heard the lid of the ashcan rattle outside the kitchen door.

'Where's the cat?' she asked when he came in again.

He was washing his hands at the kitchen sink. 'I don't know.' He got the floor mop and brought it into the living-room. He scrubbed the spot where the animal had lain. 'Not much blood. I don't see any here, in fact.'

While they were having breakfast, the cat came in through the front door, which Edith had opened to air the living room – although she had not noticed any smell. The cat looked at them in a tired way, barely raised her head, and said, 'Mi-o-ow,' the first sound she had uttered since her arrival.

'Good pussy!' Charles said with enthusiasm. 'Good Puss-Puss!'

But the cat ducked from under his congratulatory hand that would have stroked her back and went on slowly into the kitchen for her breakfast of tuna.

Charles glanced at Edith with a smile which she tried to return. She had barely finished her egg, but could not eat a bite more of her toast.

She took the car and did her shopping in a fog, greeting

familiar faces as she always did, yet she felt no contact between herself and other people. When she came home, Charles was lying on the bed, fully dressed, his hands behind his head.

'I wondered where you were,' Edith said.

'I felt drowsy. Sorry.' He sat up.

'Don't be sorry. If you want a nap, take one.'

'I was going to get the cobwebs out of the garage and give it a good sweeping.' He got to his feet. 'But aren't you glad it's gone, dear — whatever it was?' he asked, forcing a laugh.

'Of course. Yes, God knows.' But she still felt depressed, and she sensed that Charlie did, too. She stood hesitantly in the doorway. 'I just wonder what it was.' If we'd only seen the head, she thought, but couldn't say it. Wouldn't the head turn up, inside or outside the house? The cat couldn't have eaten the skull.

'Something like a ferret,' Charles said. 'We can give the cat back now, if you like.'

But they decided to wait till tomorrow to ring the Farrows.

Now Puss-Puss seemed to smile when Edith looked at her. It was a weary smile, or was the weariness only in the eyes? After all, the cat was nine. Edith glanced at the cat many times as she went about her chores that weekend. The cat had a different air, as if she had done her duty and knew it, but took no particular pride in it.

In a curious way Edith felt that the cat was in alliance with the yuma, or whatever animal it had been — was or had been in alliance. They were both animals and had understood each other, one the enemy and stronger, the other the prey. And the cat had been able to see it, perhaps hear it too, and had been able to get her claws into it. Above all, the cat was not afraid as she was, and even Charles was, Edith felt. At the same time she was thinking this, Edith realized that she disliked the cat. It had a gloomy, secretive look. The cat didn't really like them, either.

Edith had intended to phone the Farrows around three on Sunday afternoon, but Charles went to the telephone himself and told Edith he was going to call them. Edith dreaded hearing even Charles's part of the conversation, but she sat on with the Sunday papers on the sofa, listening.

Charles thanked them profusely and said the cat had caught something like a large squirrel or a ferret. But they really didn't want to keep the cat, nice as she was, and could they bring her over, say around six? 'But – well, the job's done, you see, and we're awfully grateful . . . I'll definitely ask at the plant if there's anyone who'd like a nice cat.'

Charles loosened his collar after he put the telephone down. 'Whew! That was tough – I felt like a heel! But after all, there's no use saying we want the cat when we don't. Is there?'

'Certainly not. But we ought to take them a bottle of wine or something, don't you think?'

'Oh, definitely. What a good idea! Have we got any?'

They hadn't any. There was nothing in the way of unopened drink but a bottle of whisky, which Edith proposed cheerfully.

'They did do us a big favour,' Edith said.

Charles smiled. 'That they did!' He wrapped the bottle in one of the green tissues in which their liquor store delivered bottles and set out with Puss-Puss in her basket.

Edith had said she did not care to go, but to be sure to give her thanks to the Farrows. Then Edith sat down on the sofa and tried to read the newspapers, but found her thoughts wandering. She looked around the empty, silent room, looked at the foot of the stairs and through the dining-room door.

It was gone now, the yuma baby. Why she thought it was a baby, she didn't know. A baby *what*? But she had always thought of it as young – and at the same time as cruel, and knowing about all the cruelty and evil in the world, the animal world and the human world. And its neck had been severed by a cat. They had not found the head.

She was still sitting on the sofa when Charles came back.

He came into the living-room with a slow step and slumped into the armchair. 'Well – they didn't exactly want to take her back.'

'What do you mean?'

'It isn't their cat, you know. They only took her on out of kindness – or something – when the people next door left. They were going to Australia and couldn't take the cat with them. The cat sort of hangs around the two houses there, but the Farrows feed her. It's sad.'

Edith shook her head involuntarily. 'I really didn't like the cat. It's too old for a new home, isn't it?'

'I suppose so. Well, at least she isn't going to starve with the Farrows. Can we have a cup of tea, do you think? I'd rather have that than a drink.'

And Charles went to bed early, after rubbing his right shoulder with liniment. Edith knew he was afraid of his bursitis or rheumatism starting.

'I'm getting old,' Charles said to her. 'Anyway, I feel old tonight.'

So did Edith. She also felt melancholy. Standing at the bathroom mirror she thought the little lines under her eyes looked deeper. The day had been a strain, for a Sunday. But the horror was out of the house. That was something. She had lived under it for nearly a fortnight.

Now that the yuma was dead, she realized what the trouble had been, or she could now admit it. The yuma had opened up the past, and it had been like a dark and frightening gorge. It had brought back the time when she had lost her child – on purpose – and it had recalled Charles's bitter chagrin then, his pretended indifference later. It had brought back her guilt. And she wondered if the animal had done the same thing to Charles? He hadn't been entirely noble in his early days at Pan-Com. He had told the truth about a man to a superior, the man had been dismissed – Charles had got his job – and the man had later committed suicide. Simpson. Charles had shrugged at the time. But had the yuma reminded him of Simpson? No person, no adult in the world, had a perfectly honourable past, a past without some crime in it . . .

Less than a week later, Charles was watering the roses one

evening when he saw an animal's face in the hole of the bird-house. It was the same face as the other animal's, or the face Edith had described to him, though he had never had such a good look at it as this.

There were the bright, fixed black eyes, the grim little mouth, the terrible alertness of which Edith had told him. The hose, forgotten in his hands, shot water straight out against the brick wall. He dropped the hose, and turned toward the house to cut the water off, intending to take the birdhouse down at once and see what was in it; but, he thought at the same time, the birdhouse wasn't big enough to hold such an animal as Puss-Puss had caught. That was certain.

Charles was almost at the house, running, when he saw Edith standing in the doorway.

She was looking at the birdhouse, 'There it is *again*!'

'Yes.' Charles turned off the water. 'This time I'll see what it is.'

He started for the birdhouse at a trot, but midway he stopped, staring toward the gate.

Through the open iron gate came Puss-Puss, looking be-draggled and exhausted, even apologetic. She had been walking, but now she trotted in an elderly way toward Charles, her head hanging.

'She's back,' Charles said.

A fearful gloom settled on Edith. It was all so ordained, so terribly predictable. There would be more and more yumas. When Charles shook the birdhouse in a moment, there wouldn't be anything in it, and then she would see the animal in the house, and Puss-Puss would again catch it. She and Charles, together, were stuck with it.

'She found her way all the way back here, I'm sure. Two miles,' Charles said to Edith, smiling.

But Edith clamped her teeth to repress a scream.

MORE ABOUT PENGUINS, PELICANS, AND PUFFINS

For further information about books available from Penguins please write to Dept EP, Penguin Books Ltd, Harmondsworth, Middlesex UB7 0DA.

In the U.S.A.: For a complete list of books available from Penguins in the United States write to Dept DG, Penguin Books, 299 Murray Hill Parkway, East Rutherford, New Jersey 07073.

In Canada: For a complete list of books available from Penguins in Canada write to Penguin Books Canada Ltd, 2801 John Street, Markham, Ontario L3R 1B4.

In Australia: For a complete list of books available from Penguins in Australia write to the Marketing Department, Penguin Books Australia Ltd, P.O. Box 257, Ringwood, Victoria 3134.

In New Zealand: For a complete list of books available from Penguins in New Zealand write to the Marketing Department, Penguin Books (N.Z.) Ltd, Private Bag, Takapuna, Auckland 9.

In India: For a complete list of books available from Penguins in India write to Penguin Overseas Ltd, 706 Eros Apartments, 56 Nehru Place, New Delhi 110019.

Patricia Highsmith in Penguins

THE TALENTED MR RIPLEY

'What was he doing at twenty-five? Living from week to week? No bank account. Dodging cops now for the first time in his life.'

Ripley wanted out. Wanted money, success – the good life. Was willing to kill for it.

'As haunting and harrowing a study of a schizophrenic murderer as paper will bear' – *Sunday Times*

RIPLEY UNDER GROUND

To avoid charges of forgery, the Buckmaster Gallery must produce the British artist, Derwatt. But he, unfortunately, is dead.

Tom Ripley is the only man who can perform the miraculous – and who will stop at nothing, including murder.

RIPLEY'S GAME

Tom Ripley detested murder. Unless it was absolutely neccessary. If possible, he preferred someone else to do the dirty work. In this case, someone with no criminal record, who would commit 'two simple murders' for a very generous fee.

Patricia Highsmith in Penguins

PEOPLE WHO KNOCK ON THE DOOR

A Calvinist cavalry is sweeping through America's soul.

As the Evangelical revival tightens its hold on the Mid-West, its deep conservatism, backed by financial interest, is investing heavily in the weak, the frightened, the disturbed.

When Richard Alderman becomes a born-again Christian, his teenage son Arthur's opposition creates an implacable hostility between them. And when his other son adopts his father's views, the ensuing turmoil of deceit unveils disconcerting notions of justice . . .

Patricia Highsmith pitilessly dissects the prying suburban self-righteousness which leads to frenzies for which ultimately we all must pay.

'She has an uncanny feeling for the rhythms of terror . . . a great gift to create excitement out of apprehension' – *The Times Literary Supplement*

'Venomously accurate' – *Sunday Times*

Also published

THE CRY OF THE OWL

DEEP WATER

A DOG'S RANSOM

EDITH'S DIARY

THE GLASS CELL

LITTLE TALES OF MISOGYNY

STRANGERS ON A TRAIN

A SUSPENSION OF MERCY

THIS SWEET SICKNESS

M.M. Kaye in Penguins

DEATH IN KENYA

A masterpiece of mystery and romance by the bestselling author of *The Far Pavilions* and *Death in Zanzibar*.

Lady Emily DeBrett loves her beautiful Kenyan estate, *Flamingo*, more, it could be said, than life itself . . . Under her forceful personality life in the Rift Valley is recovering uneasily from the Mau Mau terrorist uprising. But for the small white community at *Flamingo* there are further terrors as a new danger now stalks among the pepper trees and jacarandas. For this time the murderer is in their midst . . .

'A most exciting mystery story' – *Yorkshire Post*

DEATH IN ZANZIBAR

To Dany Ashton it seems like the offer of the holiday of a lifetime when her stepfather invites her to stay on the exotic 'Isle of Cloves'. But even before her plane takes off Dany's delight has faded as she finds herself at the centre of a frightening mystery. On her arrival at *Kivulimi*, the 'House of Shade', her unease turns to terror when she realizes that among the houseguests is a dangerous and ruthless murderer. Dany doesn't know who to trust . . .

'I recommend it wholeheartedly to those who fancy the idea of Agatha Christie with a touch of romantic suspense' – Auberon Waugh in the *Standard*